T0357301

# LAST
# CHANCE
# TO
# SAVE
# THE WORLD

# LAST CHANCE TO SAVE THE WORLD

## BETH REVIS

**DAW BOOKS**

NEW YORK

This is a work of fiction. Names, characters, places, and incidents are products of the author's imagination or are used fictitiously. Any resemblance to actual events, locales, or persons, living or dead, is entirely coincidental.

Jacket design by Adam Auerbach
Book design by Fine Design
Edited by Navah Wolfe
DAW Book Collectors No. 1980

DAW Books
An imprint of Astra Publishing House
dawbooks.com
DAW Books and its logo are registered trademarks of
Astra Publishing House

Printed in the United States of America

Library of Congress Cataloging-in-Publication Data is available upon request

ISBN 9780756419707 (hardcover)
ISBN 9780756419714 (ebook)

First edition: April 2025
10  9  8  7  6  5  4  3  2  1

## EPIGRAPH

The epigraph of this book is the ineffable
(and obviously unquotable)
attitude of a Canadian goose.

# UNITED GALACTIC SYSTEM

---

*Externally Sourced Communication Network*
**EMERGENCY CLEARANCE: OR-3243**
**ENCRYPTION CODE: X3GQW4PBEFIJK**
**SUBJECT: URGENT—CLIMATE-CLEANER PROGRAM**
**MARKED: TOP SECRET**

I'm sure you all noticed that I left the gala somewhat abruptly[1] and not according to the planned agenda. I will not be going into the details of my departure,[2] but please know that I have since come into some information, which I believe to be true, about the upcoming release of the climate changers.

Due to the sensitive nature of the situation, I will not be disclosing more[3] at this time.

I *will* be in attendance of the launch of the nanobots in Sol-Earth's atmosphere.

I will be accompanied by a civilian, Ada Jane Lamarr.

I know all of you are aware of Lamarr's past and my interactions with her in regards to the mission at the UGS *Roundabout*. You were all briefed about the possibility of her

---

1 I really hope that drug Ada gave me didn't make me say or do anything too stupid on the way out.

2 Although apparently at least one member of my team already knew, based on what Ada's let slip. I'm not sure who, though.

3 At least not until I'm certain this message gets through to the right people.

interference prior to the gala, when the guest list was released and security teams were developed.

You know that Ada Lamarr is a security risk.[4]

However, she has access to information that is *imperative* to the successful launch of the nanobot climate-cleaner program. Therefore, please disregard all directives previously stated in regards to Lamarr.

Prior to the release of the nanobots, you are **_not_** to interfere with myself or Lamarr. Do not approach, do not engage in conversation.[5]

Unfortunately, despite the fact that Lamarr has provided valuable information to me in regards to a secure situation, it is clear that she knows more than she has told me, and it is patently evident that her plans are not altruistic.

I have collected enough evidence to bring her into custody.

**REPEAT:** Prior to the release of the nanobots, you are **_not_** to interfere.[6]

However, once the nanobots are released into the environment, apprehending Lamarr will be our top target.[7]

---

4  To put it nicely.

5  Much as I hate to admit it, I do trust Ada here. I believe her. The nanobots need to be reprogrammed before release, and it's going to be tricky doing it without being caught. I need her help. I need my team to not interfere before then.

6  If she runs . . . I know she's skilled enough to disappear. And take the proper coding for the climate-cleaner nanobots with her.

7  She knows so much—contacts in the underworld, higher levels of knowledge than some people on my team.

I am aware of the sensitive nature of the plans involved in the climate-cleaner launch.[8] Lamarr and I will be in Fetor Towers during the launch, and apprehension at that location is not preferred.[9]

I will ensure Lamarr and I are both in Triumph Square for the celebrations following the nanobot release.[10] At that time, move in. Lamarr is to be arrested on charges of kidnapping.[11] I will lead the investigation and interrogation of the criminal.[12]

I should not need to reiterate[13] that Lamarr is highly skilled in escape.

Every available agent needs to move in with utmost discretion to ensure the target is apprehended. *Do not let her see you in advance; we cannot risk her running.*

I am unsure of whether or not I'll be able to make contact after this message. The strategy and timeline *must* be strictly adhered to:

1. No contact until after the release of the nanobots in the system. I have no continued access to any communication unit

---

8  I should be. I wrote most of them.

9  Not only will this event be recorded for the entire galaxy to stream, live, this is also a historic event. The more we can keep this situation contained, the better.

10  Which I also helped organize. I know every agent assigned to security on the square, and I personally checked the grid layout of all the surveillance drones.

11  I'm never going to live down the fact that she kidnapped *me*.

12  At least I have some negotiation room. I can arrest her and offer to drop charges if she'll tell me more. She won't cooperate unless I have a sword over her head; I know that much for certain.

13  And yet, I do.

currently, and in-person communication should not be attempted.

2. Inform no one else of these plans. Consider these commands under N2K-42.[14]

3. Be in position around Triumph Square.[15] Plainclothes. If Ada Lamarr has ever seen your face, do not get into position until after the scheduled launch to minimize her chance of recognizing you.

4. Move in *immediately* after. Lamarr will likely be close to me, but she *will* run.[16]

5. After arrest, take her immediately to the secure interrogation room.

The target is unlikely to cause physical harm,[17] but[18] she will not want to be apprehended.[19]

---

14  Top security, no acknowledgement. Ada won't tell me who the leak is, so I cannot afford to trust anyone but my closest agents.

15  We have to get through with the reprogramming before we arrest her. If my people are ready to arrest in Fetor Tech, there's too great a chance of either tipping Ada off or my team moving in too early. Fixing the malicious code in the bots is more important than arresting Ada and gaining whatever information we can from her.

16  Or have some other plan. I don't think she knows that I have a communication access point here on the station, but she might. She's always been one step ahead of me. My only hope is that she trusts me enough to believe I wouldn't turn her in.

17  Except to me. She's going to fucking murder me when she realizes I betrayed her.

18  . . . and maybe I would deserve it.

19  This is going to get messy.

# 1

I watch as Rian strides across the docking bay platform, straight to the onboard ramp at the back of *Glory*. He walks as if he has never once doubted gravity, as if the surety of landing on solid ground is a guarantee so irrevocable, it never even occurs to him to question it.

This little layover on the Moon—capital M because it's the original, the one circling Earth, the other original—was expected, but the delays are absolutely not helping my stress levels. I've spent most of the last three hours wrangling with the port authority to get the landing sequence I want. Letting Rian out of my sight was a risk but one I had to take.

Rian draws up short when he sees me opposite the ramp, leaning against the wall of the cargo bay.

"I just went for . . ." he says weakly, holding up a bag of snacks he must have purchased in the common area.

My eyes rake over him. After the initial shock of being kidnapped followed by the secondary shock of me explaining *why* the kidnapping was genius on my part, actually, Rian's been pretty compliant. Sure, he wasn't *thrilled* I turned our first date into a felony, but he definitely agrees with me that the nanobots Fetor Tech is going to be releasing on the intergalactic government's dime and approval need to be reprogrammed first, and this is the most expedient way to do it.

He knows how important this mission is. He knows that what I'm doing is designed to help all the billions of people on my ravaged planet.

Still.

That man is a rule-follower, through and through. And if there's one thing I've learned, it's that you can never trust people who trust the law.

I blow a breath of air out through my lips, shaking my head softly at him. "I wish you would have just slept with me when you had the chance," I say.

The bag of blue puff cubes drops to the floor with a soft *thwump.* "Ada—" he starts, and then seems incapable of saying anything past my name.

I bite the corner of my lip. His eyes fall south, his gaze a knife-point at the place where my teeth press into the sensitive skin.

I cross the cargo bay toward him, slamming my hand on the ramp riser button before I do. Rian doesn't even look as *Glory's* onboard ramp lifts and seals shut into the wall.

I stalk closer to him, and he fumbles backward, eyes wide, like a prey caught in a predator's path. I don't stop until his lean shoulders hit the solid metal wall paneling of my ship. When my toes are centimeters from his, I shift my body forward, my hands flat against the wall on either side of his face.

I'm so close to him that I can only take in a piece of him at a time. His warm hazel eyes, open wide and practically vibrating with anticipation. His tongue flicking out, licking his bottom lip. The faint flush creeping up his cheeks. His Adam's apple bobbing as he swallows.

I tip forward. An unsteady position, but he's seen me in worse. He's put me in worse.

I can feel his breath, sweet from blue puff cubes.

"Close your eyes," I say

He does. Instantly. His breath catches.

I dip my lips to his ear, licking the delicate shell of it before nibbling on the lobe. He groans, the sound guttural, and I wonder if—*finally*—I've taken the gravity out from under him.

"Don't you realize?" I whisper, watching as the little hairs on the back of his neck prickle. "We had a whole week in the portal pathway to get to Earth. Don't you know how much we could have done with a whole week?"

"Ada," he says, more moan than word.

Then his eyes clear.

"Ada," he says again, sharper now. "I'm not going to sleep with someone who *kidnaps me*."

"Oh my god, are you still on that? It was one time."

"It was literally this week! I am currently still in the process of *being kidnapped!*"

I roll my eyes. "You take the fun out of everything."

I head toward the bridge. I know he'll follow. "There's one bed on this spaceship, Rian, *one bed.* Plus, I can turn gravity off whenever I want. Have you ever had sex without gravity, because let me tell you, fucking *amazing.*"

"I—er—" His words trip more than his feet as he tries to keep up with the quick pace I set. "I didn't know that was an option!"

I roll my eyes. "I thought you were smart."

"Ada, we're trying to save the world; we don't have time to—"

"Well, not *now,*" I snap back, spinning on my heel to glare at him. "You have had every chance to sleep with me, and you didn't, and now you don't get to."

He looks aghast, and that does wonders for my confidence. "You mean . . ." I can see the chaos in his eyes, the confusion that I had just been all sexy-ear-nibbling and now am telling him he lost his chance for some *very* exciting times. I can almost see the words he doesn't say: *Because you don't want me anymore?*

I let him linger with that for a second. He deserves to have a little angst.

"Because," I finally say, "we've got our landing sequence, dumbass. I like sex to be adventurous, but not burning-through-the-atmosphere-of-Earth-during-reentry adven-turous."

I pause. "Huh. I guess I do have some limits."

I pause again. "Or . . ." My eyes trail over Rian's body.

*"No,"* he says emphatically.

"Oh, come on. Aren't you curious? It could be fun."

"It could be deadly. I am absolutely *not* going to have sex while *Glory* is rocketing toward a *planet*."

I jut my bottom lip out, mostly to watch the way Rian tries not to look at it. "I keep telling you not to be boring, and you never listen."

Turning back around, I step into the bridge and head straight to my pilot seat. "We had literally nothing else to do the entire time in the portal," I grumble.

"You mean aside from plotting to break into the most se-cure building on the planet and fuck some shit up?" Rian asks.

"Aside from that."

We've developed a good plan. It's the whole reason why I had to kidnap Rian in the first place. Over the past week, while the man's been oblivious to any physical activities we could have been doing, we've gone over every schematic of Fetor Towers, mapped out the exact paths needed to get to the nanobot programming unit, and I've been perfecting the code I'm replacing within the bots.

It's painfully simple. Rian's the only government employee sympathetic to the cause and who also has high-enough clearance to be right beside Fetor during the launch. I'm going to be his guest. Not technically on the list, but we'll push through. Rian will be expected to leave me behind, with the less-important people and media, while he ascends to the penthouse of Fetor Towers.

I will, of course, not be doing that.

It's a fucking *tight* timeline, made more complicated by the fact that I've been held up longer on the Moon station than I anticipated. And getting the landing sequence I need was a pain in the ass.

But we're moving now.

I can hear Rian settling into the jump seat behind me; the metal clicks as he adjusts the harness. "I didn't even know you were trying to seduce me!"

Heh. He's still on that.

I toss him my flattest look. "I could not have been more obvious."

"You absolutely could have been more obvious," Rian says, fumbling for the harness. "As evidenced by—"

"Your obliviousness?" I offer.

Rian sputters as he straps in.

"Anyway, step one: complete," I say.

"Step one in . . . seduction?"

"No. You missed that chance. First step to saving the world," I remind him.

Our timeline starts tomorrow. Rian and I both agreed

that we would need to get into the building only hours before the nanobots designed to clean up Earth's climate are released. If we try to do it any sooner, it would mean that both (a) it would look suspicious that Rian came so far ahead of schedule and (b) someone could spot the changes we made and revert back to Fetor's programming—the programming that would mean the bots would critically fail and leave the entirety of the planet at the mercy of one asshole trillionaire.

So, we go in tomorrow.

But before that, I had to get permission to dock my ship in the most secure landing strip on Earth.

And, because I'm fucking amazing, I did just that. Despite the fact that we had to wait for-fucking-ever to get it. I expected some delays, but this has been ridiculous.

"I got the clearance codes to land near Malta," I tell Rian with exactly the right amount of smugness that little feat deserves.

Malta: the small island nation in the Mediterranean that was once home to the first global government. Revolutions shook some of that up, and so did the shift from true governing influence to the unholy alliance between taxes and tourism boards, but Malta's still culturally important. And, more to the point, the home of Fetor Tech, where the nanobots are going to be launched.

Although the launch of the climate-cleaner program and

all the high-security red tape around it did mean we've spent longer on the Moon than I intended.

"Do all these delays mess with the timeline? It's really cutting things close," Rian says. I'm pretty sure all the officials invited to the launch of the nanobots are already in the city. They didn't have to arrange for clearance codes or anything like that.

I don't like the timing either, but there's not much I can do about it. "We'll still have plenty of time," I think, calculating that for myself as much as for him.

But that's not true, is it? A running list flashes through my mind—get inside the building, get past security into the room where the bots are, get the code uploaded, get to the other office, do the thing Rian doesn't know about, and get out without getting caught . . . by Fetor's people or Rian's.

I press a few buttons on my ship's console, and *Glory* starts battening down the hatches. I assume. Where did that term come from? Anyway, my ship's priming for launch.

"I could have pulled some strings," Rian reminds me. "Gotten us a private relay or something."

This is dangerous. This plan. And Rian's connections would have made it easier, obviously.

"I don't like strings," I say, perhaps a little too sharply.

Good thing he doesn't know I have some connections of my own.

# 2

"This is never going to work," Rian mutters.

"Not with that attitude," I say cheerily.

It doesn't take long for us to clear the Moon's station and head toward that blue marble. From here, the planet still looks healthy and glowing. Clouds swirl over vast oceans. I know from research that the beauty of Earth has dimmed over time. Even those grainy original photos from the first few flights into space promised more life than now. From here, I can see dark spots in the ocean where islands of trash float, large enough to support colonies of rovers. More brown swaths across the continents than a millennium ago, and far, far less white.

But at least from this distance, it's possible to pretend the world doesn't need saving, that the fate of an entire planet doesn't rest on the bits of code I've been writing and rewriting and tinkering with for the past week. Well, actually— it's not the fate of the planet. It's the fate of humanity living on the planet. Because I have no doubt Earth will continue on after the last human. And maybe would be better without the parasites.

As we get closer to Earth, I twist around in the pilot seat to see Rian. *Glory* is not made for mild conversation while burning through the atmosphere of a nearly dead planet, but I've had worse landing situations. Besides, I'm comfortable in my nest, every control perfectly fitted to my body.

I know how this bird flies.

"Eyes up front!" Rian shouts. From this angle, I can't see if his knuckles are white, but there's no mistaking how tense he is.

"You are absolutely adorable when you're terrified for your life," I say, unable to keep the infatuation from my voice.

"Could you *please*, for the love of all things holy, stay focused?"

Rian is definitely not comfortable flying. I noticed it before, when we first met, but it's very obvious in this moment. Which, now that I think of it is, isn't really very polite, is it? When the crew of the *Halifax* was shuttling him to the protoplanet's surface, he kept his mouth shut and his nerves tamped down.

*Maybe it's because he feels safe enough with me to show his true feelings,* I think.

Behind me, I hear a suspicious gagging sound. I lean back, eyeballing him again. "You had better not vomit in my ship. You're cute but not cute enough for that."

Rian's jaw works as he frantically points to the front of the ship. Sighing, I turn back around. He's acting as if I need to keep my eyes on the road, but there *is* no road when you're reentering a planet's atmosphere, and besides, there's no point looking out the window right now. If anything, I suppose I should look at the controls in front of me, and . . .

Oh, shit.

That switch shouldn't be flipped that way. *Shit.* I flick it with my forefinger and then pull up on the throttle. *Glory* judders, an alarm sounds three times before I silence it, and Rian makes another funny sound followed by a lot of cursing.

*Glory's* gravity generator is working overtime to counter some of the g-forces in landing, but it's still a strain to hold my body so I can turn and see Rian. "It's fine," I tell him.

"The ship is on *fire*," he says. No need for the yelling, damn.

"That's normal."

It is. It *is*. Reentry requires burn-off. Yes, there's fire, but it's all outside. Which is, by far, the preferable place for a fire to be when you're inside.

"Have you never seen a ship burn through atmo?" I ask.

Problem is, going at regular speed from the Moon to Earth takes days. We don't have days, so I'm having to use a temporary portal well and make up for it with the ship's grav gens.

It's a bit rocky, sure, but quick.

"Every time I've ever been on a ship landing on a planet with atmosphere, I've been strapped in a passenger seat." One with vid screens instead of windows, I presume. Even at a leisurely cruise pace, there's still burn-off.

"Sitting neat and proper like a good little boy," I say. Shit, I really should have flipped that one switch sooner. Silencing the alarm did make the noise go away, but that wasn't a fantastic time to lapse in judgement.

"I'm not a good little—"

"I know. You could stand to be a little naughtier. We discussed that already."

*"You kidnapped me!"* Rian bellows. "And now we're heading to fucking Sol-Earth in a ship that is on *fire!*"

Fine. He's not in the mood to talk. You'd think he would settle down after a while, but no. He's still pissed I happened to take him *somewhat* against his will.

Even if it's for a good cause.

"You're going to have to get over the kidnapping thing eventually," I grouse.

*Glory* lurches, and my stomach does a little swoop as the grav generators catch up to reentry and the ship evens out.

"See? Nothing to worry about." I shoot Rian my best winning smile, which does absolutely nothing to him. His mouth is a tight line as I toss aside my harness and turn to look at him. Autopilot is on now, and I can't really do anything until I get the landing coordinates.

I lean forward, no mean feat, given our relative positions in the cramped bridge. "So," I say, "let's talk plans."

Rian sucks in air and lets it out so forcefully that his nostrils flare.

"Okay, *fine,* we can have the argument again," I say somewhat impatiently, "but we both know that in the end, you're going to agree with me. Because I'm right. And you know it."

"I know," Rian says, and when I shoot him a look, he says it with more conviction. "I *know.* You're right."

God, he's hot when he says that. Music to my ears.

A red light starts blinking on my console.

Rian frowns at it. "Do you need to—"

"No, it's fine. Let's talk more about how I'm right."

Rian gives me a glare. "I see the point you made. I can even concede that . . ." He looks around at *Glory*'s bridge. "That extreme measures are needed."

"See? Even kidnapping has a place."

Rian pinches his nose. "It's just . . ."

"No." I shake my head forcefully. "What we're *not* going to do right now is second-guess the plan. The plan is good."

"Fine," he snaps. Grumpy. Ugh. He would be so much more relaxed if he had bothered being seduced. Rian looks around. "What are we doing right now?"

I also look around, confused. "Waiting to land."

We broke orbit, burned through atmo, but the landing

sequence that will take us directly to the port will have to be linked to us from the ground. So what's his issue?

Oh—I get it. Rian's not used to waiting. Passenger ships, especially cruisers, and government business gets priority.

*Glory* is not priority.

"Could be five minutes, could be an hour or two," I say. "Depends on the Maltese port boss and their order of ops."

"How did you even get landing codes close to Malta? I helped *write* the port orders for that sector. No ship can land anywhere near the island without prior authorization for this entire month."

"Yeah," I say. "I have that."

"You have . . ."

"That. Prior authorization. I have that."

Rian shakes his head. "I inspected the docking manifest myself. Your ship wasn't on it."

"I don't know why you're questioning my methods now," I say. I turn back to the console, flicking a button to turn off the red flashing light. Very distracting. "I clearly have the means to do what I want."

"Yes, but—"

The red blinking light is replaced with a beeping.

"Well, that was quicker than expected," I mutter.

"What was?" Rian's all tense again as he sees me strap back into the seat, the foot pedals rising at my touch as I lean in to the controls. "What's wrong?"

"Nothing's wrong," I say. "But look, I'm going to need you to shut up and be cool for like ten minutes."

"What does that—"

"Shut up," I say, command now in my voice. "And be cool."

I throw a glance over my shoulder. Apparently, *be cool* means *sit ramrod straight with every muscle taut*, but at least the *shut up* directive is easier for him to handle.

I flick the comm control on my ship's dash and speak into the mic. "5O213-LN, request to land at Gozo residency strip. Callsign *Glory*."

Over my comm unit's speakers, a crackling voice says, "*Glory*, confirm code."

I hear a tiny intake of breath from Rian, but he doesn't break my order.

I rattle off the numbers.

Several minutes pass.

"This isn't going to work," Rian mutters.

A few more minutes.

And then the operator links me to a landing sequence. I set *Glory*'s course, then turn back around to Rian.

"See?" I say. "It worked. I had a plan."

His lips twist in a wry smirk. "You always do, huh?"

"Would you believe me if I told you that I'm mostly just winging it?"

Rian's left eye twitches. "Yes," he says. "I would. And

considering what we're doing is going to impact the entire fate of this planet—and I'm risking my job and *prison* to do it? That's not a comforting thought."

I shoot him a winning smile and then have to turn my attention to landing *Glory*. But really, he's exaggerating. Prison? Unlikely. I mean, technically he shouldn't sneak me into Fetor Tech, but we're not stealing anything. Well, he isn't. We're not even fucking anything up. We're just making sure the code on the nanobots is the *right* code. And the only one who could theoretically press charges would be Strom Fetor himself, and if he did so, (a) he'd have to confess to altering the original code into malware that harmed the world, and (b) he'd also have to be less of a dumbass. Neither of which is likely.

Rian's still muttering about how the landing strips aren't supposed to take new ships now. It's distracting, but at least he's not making noises that make me worried he's going to throw up all over my bridge, so I don't comment.

He's right. It's not entirely uncommon for Malta's landing strips to be restricted. There are enough important governmental things happening in the capital still for there to be a lot of regulations, and regulations are generally a pain in the ass.

*Glory*'s speakers flash—incoming transmission. "*Glory,* you're required to check in with the residency strip port boss upon arrival."

"Got it," I say, then close the comm.

I adjust the controls. There's more work to do in the last minutes of flying a ship before landing than in the week it took to get us here.

"Residency?" Rian asks.

Fuck it all, of course he would notice that. One word. If the port authority hadn't said that one word, he might not have picked up on it.

"I looked into all your records," he presses. "You don't own land anywhere, and there's no rental record for you."

"I'm a lady of mystery," I say, half-distracted by my tight grip on the joysticks, both of which are doing their best to rip my arms off.

He makes a harrumphing noise in the back of his throat.

"Oh, ye of little faith," I say, laughing in a tone that's only a little forced. "You didn't think we'd even get this far, did you?"

I can see the white caps of the waves as *Glory* soars over the Mediterranean before I hear his less-than-comforting response:

"You're not the only one with backup plans."

# 3

The landing strips are roughly fifty kilometers from the island. There are two—a large one for cruisers carrying tourists and rich people, and a much smaller one for locals with residency or transports carrying cargo for delivery. The large strip has passenger boarding bridges that go up to the cruisers, letting guests get off in an enclosed, air-conditioned tube that deposits them in a luxurious building at the end of the dock that connects directly to the ferry that transports people from the strips to Malta. Not a single drop of sunlight gets through either the bridge or the building, although they're lined with vid screens displaying immaculate blue waves and clear skies at all times.

The residency strip doesn't bother lying. When Rian and I step out onto the main dock, the sun beats down on us, and the stench of the gray water fills our nostrils.

"Ada Lamarr!" a voice calls down the strip. I whirl around. "Bruna?"

A large woman strides toward me, wrapping me up in an

enormous hug. "Where you been?" she says, the words so deep I can feel them vibrating from her chest to mine.

I push her back, laughing. "It's been forever!" And then I glance at her uniform. "*You're* the port boss?"

She beams at me, then notices Rian hanging back awkwardly. "And who is this?"

Before I can say anything, Rian steps forward, hand out, and introduces himself. Bruna shakes it earnestly, then looks at me, eyebrows raised. "Lover?"

Rian gapes at her.

"No, but only because he's an idiot," I say.

"I am not!"

I give him a look that clearly says, *We had a* week, *and you didn't make a single move.*

"Okay, maybe I'm an idiot," Rian grumbles.

Bruna laughs.

"We were in university together," I tell Rian.

"But you didn't graduate." The words slip past his lips before he thinks to stop them, and I can tell that he didn't mean to say it like that, like an insult.

It would sting, but that's an old wound. The nerves are long dead.

Bruna slings an arm around my shoulders. "Not because she wasn't smart enough! They should have given her the diploma."

I shrug, and Bruna takes the hint, dropping her hold on me. Bruna knows why I gave up on higher education, because she was right there beside me until the end. And Rian knows because he snooped in my history. A bit of a criminal record following a spot of hacking and vandalism after her father's untimely death due to climate sickness can throw a girl off track in her education and make the university withhold credits due to "unbefitting behavior for a student." Turns out admin frowns on using the skills they teach you for anything fun.

"Anyway," I say, desperate to change the subject. Maybe there is still a little pain left in that scar.

"Your mother pinged before you landed," Bruna says

Fuck.

Rian's head snaps up at that. I know he knew about my father, but he definitely didn't note much about my mother. And that was by extremely careful design.

*Shut your gob, Bruna,* I think.

Bruna does not, in fact, shut her gob. Instead, she says, "She told me to tell you to come straight by for a visit."

Shit.

Shit, shit, triple shit.

"Don't glare at me," Bruna protests, throwing up her hands. "I'm only delivering the message."

"Well, deliver another message for me, will ya? Tell Mom I don't have time for a visit this round."

"Tell her yourself. I'm not getting in the middle of it. Besides, you have to go."

I blink. "*Have* to?"

"All residents have to ping their geolocation at their place of residence within three hours of landing at the Maltese strip," Rian says, likes he's reading the words out of a codex.

Fucking hell, this rule *reeks* of the kind of shit someone from Rigel-Earth would force into regulation. Someone like Rian Fucking White.

"Why?" I grind out.

Bruna shrugs. "Something, something security and ensuring people are actually residents if they come through on that code. Big thing happening in New Venice tomorrow."

"Oh, really?" I ask innocently, knowing full well that the "big thing" is what I'm aiming to fuck up.

Bruna shrugs. "Apparently." She nods toward the other nearby dock, the one for people with money. "They're not even allowing most cruisers. That's the last for the next three days."

"Fine," I say. "I'll go to the place listed as *Glory*'s residency, ping the geo-tracker, and then come back. Rian, you stay here—"

I stop because both Rian and Bruna look as if I've suggested the impossible.

"*Everyone* on board a ship claiming residency has to ping the tracker," Bruna says.

"Come on," I object. "I can hide him in the ship."

"I'm not hiding in the ship," Rian offers.

"It's not up to me!" Bruna protests. "You know I'd turn a blind eye, Ada, but this shit is tracked."

She holds up a data pad that displays a small chart, pointing to *Glory*'s registry number, already filled in on one side. Two codes are listed beside it—one is my ident sequence, and the other must be Rian's. Beside each of our numbers is a little timer, currently flashing yellow.

Our identities are already being tracked by the government, just for using a government-controlled landing strip.

"This is absolutely the kind of shit that belongs on Rigel-Earth, not here," I say, glaring at Rian, who at least has the sense to look a little guilty.

I force myself to take regular breaths. I should have factored all this in, but I'm so used to operating on outposts and stations that aren't as strict. I haven't been back here in years, and it shows.

It's fine. This is fine. I can make it work.

I have to.

"Are you going to the square after?" Bruna's tone is light, casual, and so opposite of the panic screaming in my head that it shakes me out of my spiral.

"They planning a party?" I ask. She's talking about Triumph Square, the large courtyard just outside of Central Gardens. Rallies, markets, and celebrations are all held there.

I've been so focused on the mission—changing the code inside the nanobots being released tomorrow—that I forgot the way it's an interplanetary event. A cause for celebration.

"Gonna be huge," she says.

I eye Rian. "Yeah, maybe we'll go." If we succeed.

"Well, I better let you get on," Bruna says, flashing the screen at us again. My eyes linger on the timer ticking away the seconds before we need to ping our location to the government.

"Oh, one more thing," Bruna says, snapping her fingers at the memory. "Jane told me to tell you specifically—"

"Jane?" Rian's voice cracks like a whip, so sharp that Bruna's eyes widen. I know exactly what he's thinking: the code word *Jane Irwin*. Let me nip that in the bud.

"Jane Lamarr, the woman who birthed me and gave me my middle name," I remind him in a deadpan voice. "It's only one of the most common names on the planet."

He has the grace to look a little embarrassed by that.

Bruna cocks an eyebrow at me, gaze flicking between us. Rian doesn't know it, but Bruna is *definitely* aware of "Jane Irwin," and I'm realizing now that it was no accident she came to me personally to deliver this message.

"Jane told me to tell you she fully expects you to spend the night."

I groan.

I don't like this; I hate this. I can *feel* Rian getting more interested in this conversation by the minute.

Why—*why*—would my mother interfere right now?

Bruna snorts. "When was the last time you brought a lover home to your mother?"

"Not since you, in the before times," I say, sticking my tongue out at her.

"Hey, we're not lovers!" Rian protests.

"Not yet," I say, and Bruna gives me an obnoxiously loud high five.

Despite my smile, I'm fuming inside. I didn't even want Rian to know that I can land on a residency strip at Malta. I don't like him knowing I have a place with permanence.

I don't like the way this narrows the world around me, the way he can cage me here, pin me down.

But what I don't like even more?

Him meeting my mother.

Bruna waves farewell as we return to *Glory* to gather supplies. Since I know that message means we're not going back to the ship any time soon, I grab a bag and start packing.

Rian doesn't have much in the way of luggage, a side effect of being kidnapped. But because I'm so considerate, he does have a spare set of nondescript standard-issue that's mostly in his size. I had to eyeball it when I was preparing. For the kidnapping. As one does. He stuffs everything into a spare rucksack I graciously donated to the cause while I prep a few of my own essentials.

"You travel light," he comments as I drop my bag on the floor.

The one thing I didn't get right was his shoes. Rian's still wearing his fancy kicks.

"You good to walk in those?" I ask.

"Mostly."

Lucky he didn't have useless silver heels at the gala I kidnapped him from.

I grab two sun shields from inside a storage locker and toss one to him. "You're gonna want that."

He starts to put it in his rucksack, but I shake my head. "You're going to want it now."

Rian looks about to protest, but then I take my shirt off. His mouth shuts as his eyes drop.

Sun shields come in a variety of styles—some are more like robes, some are body suits. The ones I've got are gossamer-thin, long-sleeved, and hooded. They work best when next to the skin, so I pull the shield over my bra and then replace my shirt over that.

Rian copies me. Once he's fully dressed again, I cross the short space between us and reach behind him, lifting up the thinner-than-paper hood and covering his head. After I adjust it, I realize that his gaze is zeroed in on me.

For the first time since I met him, Rian's eyes are soft, not razor-sharp.

Soft.

Because he's looking at me.

Somehow, this action—pulling his hood up—feels more intimate than when we were both half-naked a moment before. Alarm bells ring in my head.

I step back.

And I note the disappointed look on Rian's face.

As much as I wished we'd spent our days and nights in the portal with more enjoyable activities, it's game time now. I might have gotten a good romp out of him if we'd been able to stay on *Glory*, but now?

Now it's time to visit my mother.

*Fuck* this timing.

I take another step back and reach into my bag. "Also these," I say, plucking two pills from a bottle in the side pocket.

"Radiation preventative?" Rian asks, swallowing the tablet when I nod. A few minutes on the dock with Bruna isn't much, but if we're traipsing around the island, we'll need more.

Rian smacks his mouth against the metallic taste of the pills. I know he's not used to this. Cruisers and tours minimize the effects of radiation and other by-products of a polluted world.

I think it makes it easier for the other worlds to pretend that Earth's not as bad off as it is, when only the locals have to take pills and precautions just to live.

We head out, straight to the end of the dock. A few people are already on the transfer ferry—a heavy-duty boat with a trash-breaker spike up front to slice through the murky water.

I catch Rian scowling at the sea.

"We're going to fix it," I tell him gently. It won't be immediately, but once we have the nanobots out in the world's water cycle—with the right code—Earth is going to get better.

I hope.

Rian nods, his mouth a grim line as he finds a place to sit on the benches under the protection shields. The local ferry isn't like the cruiser transport; it doesn't try to hide reality. I scoot closer to him as the ferry waits for more people, resting my head on his shoulder as if we were lovers, my mouth close enough to his ear that no one can eavesdrop.

"What are the chances of you being spotted and stopped?" I ask. "Your friends gonna arrest me on sight?"

"You? The paragon of innocence?" Rian chuckles.

"Well, you know I'm harmless," I say, "but what about your team?"

"Relax." Rian nudges me, which does not at all make me relax. "They all saw us together at the gala. They probably assume . . . well . . ."

Phoebe does not assume that. She's on Rian's team, but she's on my side. Or, at least, my client's side. She knows the nanobots aren't coded well, and she won't stand in my way. But any of Rian's people who even suspect he didn't come on my ship willingly will cause some trouble.

And I desperately don't want any eyes on me.

My only saving grace is that no one from Rian's team will actually be in Fetor's offices for the launch of the nanobots. That's the whole reason why my client needed me to acquire Rian, he has the clearance. But they could cause trouble on the outside.

"We'll get in," Rian says.

"Why are you so confident about that?" I ask.

"Because that's the part of the plan I came up with."

And that's the very reason I'm concerned.

# 4

Both my cuff and Rian's have a little clock flashing in the corner of the display. As soon as we're in the region of my mother's home—which is linked to *Glory*'s residency code—our cuffs will ping the geo-tracker that we satisfied the rules for landing, and we're good.

The timer still displays a solid hour and a half by the time the ferry reaches the northern dock in Xlendi Bay. Technically, Malta used to have two main islands—Malta itself, as well as the northern provincial Gozo. The development of the bridge city, New Venice, connected the two islands and covered up the smaller ones between them. Most tourist stops and wealthy residences are on the larger island. Most of the workers and poorer residents live on Gozo.

As Rian and I get off the ferry, we step into a crowd of locals, some of whom may recognize me or at least link me to my mother. I set a fast pace, keeping my head down and my sun shield hood up as I steer Rian away from the people offering ride services. "We can walk," I tell him. Getting a transport will be more time and hassle than it's worth; plus, it'll draw attention.

He glances at his cuff. "Are you in a hurry?"

"We don't need additional eyes from the government on us right now." I tap the timer.

"We have plenty of time." Rian follows behind me. "This is . . . inconvenient, but in my defense, it's a fairly standard practice for a global event that's high-security, *and* I had no idea when the regulations were approved that we'd be doing . . ." He waves his hands in my general direction. "All of this."

"It's a dumbass rule that only someone who's never had to rely on public transportation and walking would think is just 'inconvenient,'" I snap. The time limits are ridiculous— if we'd missed the ferry and needed to take the next, we'd be sprinting to make it in time. But that's not why I'm mad.

Bruna's message had a veiled meaning, and the fact that my mother is *expecting* me is going to complicate everything. It's a sign things already *are* complicated. More so than usual.

The sidewalks are crowded, and we dodge around people as auto-taxis roll through the streets. Half the buildings here are boarded up; the other half are so dusty that the windows are basically useless. The glass is laced with metal to prevent theft, and most of them display brightly lit signs with promises of deals and bargains, neon flashing in a desperate attempt to distract from decay.

I glance back at Rian after we get separated by a man pushing a cart full of yellow-green cabbages that are going to need to be scrubbed with a wire brush to remove the grime building up on them. Rian has a contemplative scowl all over his face, and he almost walks right past me.

I grab his hand and pull him into an alley that opens up to a path toward the cliffs.

Malta's a Mediterranean island, but it's not a beach resort, especially not here. The gray waves crash into cliffs, not beaches, and the trail I'm taking Rian on is a bit of a hike up. Once we're away from the noise of the crowded streets, Rian says, "Well, after this, let's hire transport into New Venice."

I walk backward so I can look at him as I cross the small footbridge extending over an inlet. "You heard Bruna. My mother expects me to spend the night."

Rian laughs. "You're not twelve. You don't have to stay there."

"Okay, I confess," I say. "Going to my mother's house was not a part of Plan A, B, or C. But I can work with it. Plus, it's free."

"I can pay for a hotel." His voice is low, and I can tell he's reconsidering my countless and very obvious propositions.

"You may be able to afford a penthouse suite in New Venice, but can you afford a distraction the night before we do crime?"

His mouth opens, but nothing comes out. He follows me up the footpath and eventually says, "So, we're already on Plan D? How many plans do you have?"

His tone is light. Good. Let him think this is easy.

"Forty-two, minimum," I quip.

I may need Plan F before this is done. Plan F stands for "Fuck as much stuff up as possible and escape in the chaos." It also means dropping at least half of my goals, which will put me in debt I can't pay off and in . . . let's just say *bad* standing with my client.

"It's only . . ." Rian starts.

"What?" My voice is a little too snappy right now. Mask, mask. I can't let him see the truth, not so close to home. But my stomach hurts, and so do my back and my head, and I simply cannot seem to make myself able to concentrate where I need to concentrate.

"I looked, Ada," Rian says. "I looked at all the records."

Of course he did. "And?"

"And there was almost nothing on your mother."

The climb is getting a little steeper now. "Not everything is a conspiracy theory. You know my parents both worked in conservation. After Yellowstone exploded, Mom moved into government work before she retired. It's why she lives here."

And, as Rian knows, government workers are not as easy to access. He could have snooped, of course—he certainly has the clearance to check on almost anyone's records. But he was so focused on researching my sordid yet delightful past that he didn't veer down the paths that would have told him more about my mother's records. I hope.

We stick close to the coast, despite the stench of pollution. Once, the most expensive houses were along the shore. It was a luxury to be able to look at the ocean from your bedroom window. But that was when the water was clean and beautiful. Now the most valuable land is in the center of the island, as far away from the stink as possible.

"What's that?" Rian asks, pointing to a short, square tower right on the edge of the cliff overlooking the water.

"That's where we're going." I lead the way, taking a path that's older than anyone can remember, the stone steps up the cliff worn away in the center.

"There?"

No need to sound so incredulous.

Then again, that tower *is* ancient. "So, in the middle of the twentieth century—I can't remember when . . . The sixteen hundreds? Eighteen? Something like that. Anyway, there were pirates—"

"Pirates?" Rian says. "Like you?"

"I'm not a pirate; I have an ethical code."

"A looter's code. And looting is basically pirating."

"You have no sense of nuance. *Anyway*, they—"

"Who?" Rian asks.

"I don't know," I say, exasperated. "I know coding, not history. Anyway, *they* built a series of towers along the coast. Watchtowers. And if someone saw a pirate ship approaching, they lit a fire on top of the tower, and then the next tower over would see it, and they'd light their tower, and then the next and the next—"

"I get the picture."

"And the whole island would be on alert and ready before any pirate ship even landed." We've reached the top of the path now. "It was a decent system."

"I'm just in awe that a series of towers built in the seventeenth and/or nineteenth century is still standing."

"Well, this one is, and one more on the main island. The rest fell a long time ago. And this one isn't technically the original. It was moved as the coast eroded and then rebuilt, and it's mostly just a ship of Theseus at this point. But there are enough history nerds that Mom has a job keeping the tower up in between tours. It doesn't come with much pay, but at least the living quarters are included."

I pause at the top of the cliff to see how Rian reacts to the full view of the tower. He doesn't look nearly as impressed as he should.

"How do you get in?" he asks.

"There are some steps and a door on the other side." It was a watchtower against pirates; of course there's only one door.

I take one minute to drink it in. It's been years since I've seen this place—since I've seen Mom in person—and . . . I don't know. It feels like it may be the last time.

So much has gone wrong already, and we've not even made it to Fetor's headquarters.

I take a deep breath.

I tried living with Mom, right after I got my record clear. I tried, and I know she tried, too.

But we're just so different. She was fine staying right here for the rest of her life.

And I wanted nothing less.

But she's nobler than me. Even when my father got sick. She wasn't bitter about it, not the way I still am.

Even in a world as polluted as Earth, she still sees the value of it. The need to stay, to help, to fix everything.

I know she thinks the way I escaped is selfish. I know she doesn't approve of . . .

Of me.

"Ada?" Rian asks when he sees how I've stopped. He comes closer. "Hey," he adds at my dark look. "Penthouse suite in New Venice after this? We don't have to stay."

I shake my head.

It's too late now.

Rian follows my gaze to see the woman standing at the top of the steps, framed by the limestone doorway. Her skin is a shade darker than mine, her hair a shade lighter, hidden under a vivid purple scarf. She stands with her hands on her hips, looking down at us, her stern stance a contrast to the smile curving her lips.

Apprehension squeezes my stomach, hard.

But I turn to Rian with a huge grin. "Time to meet my mother."

# 5

Rian and I both ping the geo-trackers on our cuffs, and the timers stop with twenty whole minutes to spare. I shoot Rian a look: *See? The regulations aren't fair.*

He gives me a grudging nod, but I can also tell that he still expects to not be spending the night here. Time to rearrange that assessment in his neatly organized mind.

The outside of the tower is plain, pale brown limestone, few windows, only one door. Mom calls over to us, waving.

"Sorry about her," I mutter as we head up the steps.

Sure enough, as soon as I introduce Mom to Rian, she bustles us inside and stuffs a pastizz in his mouth before declaring that there's no way she'll allow him to waste money on a hotel tonight, and he can sleep in my old bedroom while I share with her. When he protests, she gives him another pastry and literally pats him on the head.

"I'm just so pleased to meet you!" Mom declares as Rian chokes on crumbs. "So, tell me all about yourself."

"I . . . work in conservation," he says awkwardly.

Great, so they're both starting off with lies.

"Conservation?" Mom asks. "I started my career there."

"I heard. Yellowstone."

Mom beams. "You've told him everything about me, haven't you?"

"Not quite," I say.

The main floor of the tower is on the second level, where the only door deposited us. The thick walls are plastered white, no personal decorations. Mounted along one wall are a few display cases holding artifacts—clay pots from Punic shipwreck remains found nearby, a World War II uniform, and some cannonballs. Carbonglass protects some plaster that was salvaged from the frescoes in the original tower, ancient graffiti made by bored soldiers stationed at the tower in the sixteen and/or eighteen hundreds. Or maybe later? I should know that, but history, eh.

During tours, Mom uses a holo projector to display information about the tower's cultural importance to the island. The few narrow windows cast natural light over the table Mom's set up in the middle of the room. This part of the tower is for display, kept simple and plain. Steps hidden behind doors go down to where Mom really lives on the first floor, and also up to the flat roof.

Mom chats ceaselessly, prattling off a mix of outrageous stories she thinks are entertaining and peppering in probing questions that catch Rian off guard.

"Sorry," I say, passing him a coffee. "I know she's . . . a lot."

"Who is?" Mom asks. "Me? I'm not a lot."

"I can see where you get it from," Rian tells me.

My eyes grow big. "You think *I'm* a lot?"

Mom barks in laughter.

"I'm an absolute fucking delight; that's what I am," I say.

"Well." Rian starts to stand from the table. "Thank you for the pastries."

"It sounds like you're trying to leave." Mom levels Rian with a Look. I know she's gearing up to say she's already got a full meal prepared for us and it would break her heart to be stuck with so much leftover food, but I push back my chair, the metal grating on the stone floor.

"Mind if Rian and I talk on the roof alone for a moment?" I ask Mom. She waves toward the door, a little frown marring her face, and I lead Rian up.

Xlendi Tower isn't tall—it didn't need to be. It's already on a cliff, and the soldiers at the watchtower only needed the signal fires to be seen by the next tower down the coast. One level up, and Rian and I step out onto the flat stone roof. A small ledge lower than knee height is all that warns us not to fall off, and we have to step carefully around the solar panels positioned for the best angle to collect the sun's rays. Along the north wall, a dovecote stands, the soft cooing of pigeons and the steady sound of the sea the only noise.

This is perhaps the only place on the whole island that stinks more of bird shit than pollution.

I don't bother mincing words. "Coming here wasn't the original plan, but I think we should stay."

"We could get a hotel a block away from Fetor's offices," Rian starts to protest. No doubt this is the same hotel he stayed at every time he inspected the project as it was developed.

My lips pinch tight. I don't necessarily want to pick a fight, but I also don't not want that. "On *Glory,* in the portal system, there was no way send messages off the ship. On the Moon station, well . . . I have to trust you didn't betray me when you got your blue puff cubes. I should have come with you when you went for 'snacks.'"

"Why would I—"

I march closer to him, jamming a finger into his chest. "I know you're on board with rewriting the code of the climate cleaners so we don't completely turn Earth into a pay-to-play game of survival," I say, "but I also know that I can't trust you."

"Ada, you can—"

I shake my head, jaw tight. "I absolutely cannot trust you, and you're an idiot if you think I've forgotten that for a second. Just because I want to fuck you does not mean I can trust you." I snort. "Actually, it makes the fucking part hotter."

He opens his mouth to speak, but I keep talking over

him. "Any hotel you get is probably linked to some government account that'll ping your team. Even if not, you'll have access to comms. You'll set me up."

Rian takes a step back, almost treading on a solar panel. "Ada, you're being difficult and paranoid."

"I'm being reasonable," I counter. I sigh. "I get it. You know I know a *lot* about—"

There they are.

Those razor eyes that see way, way too much.

"About my *client*," I say, refusing to give him even that much of an answer. "You know I have ins. You know I know people. Code words. What's the trap? Are you going to arrest me for kidnapping?"

"No!" he protests too quickly.

I cross my arms over my chest. "You go, if you want. But if you go to a hotel, I will think it's a trap, and I'm out. Which means you'll be fucked because I'm the one with the code to reprogram the nanobots, and we both know you can't do it."

Rian's mouth drops open at the same time one of the pigeons in the dovecote makes a loud warbling sound, which would be funny if it weren't for the fact that we're arguing, and I'm not certain I'm going to win this one, which would . . . fuck everything.

Finally, Rian says in a low voice, "If it means that much to you, fine. Fine. We'll stay here tonight."

I nod firmly. "And when we finish the job tomorrow, that's it. I'll disappear."

He doesn't say anything to that.

I take a step closer to him, close enough that he could reach out and touch me if he wanted.

"I'll disappear," I repeat in a softer voice, "and you'll let me."

I can't read his expression. I can't figure out what's happening behind those eyes, what calculations he's made, what trap he's laid.

I'm just certain he has one.

Without warning, his hand reaches up between us, grabbing mine. "What if I don't want you to disappear?"

Gently, I extract my fingers from his. He looks disappointed but maybe also a little defiant.

"It's better that way." My voice is almost a whisper. "You'll never like the way I break the laws you make."

His lips part, but he doesn't refute me.

It's a damn good thing I've not fallen for him, because between breaking laws and breaking hearts, there's only one I walk away from whole.

# 6

K nock, knock," Mom says, stepping up onto the roof. A flurry of feathers from the dovecote; the pigeons know who brings them snacks. "All well up here?"

I step away from Rian, retreating. Like a fucking coward. "Everything's fine. We'll spend the night, if you don't mind—"

"Mind? I insist!"

"—and then we'll be gone early in the morning."

"Thank you," Rian adds formally. He really does play the good little boy well. No wonder he wants me so bad.

"My pleasure!" Mom grins at us as she walks over to the birds. "Have you been showing Rian my babies?"

"They're very impressive," Rian says, even though he barely even glanced at them.

Mom makes a little noise in the back of her throat, and I know she's pleased. It's rare I bring home anyone for her to meet, rarer still for that person to even pretend interest in her damn birds.

"You've not even seen them properly yet!" Mom swings

open the dovecote door, exposing about two dozen little boxes with nests and pigeons inside. She reaches inside one cubby and scoops up a bird. "They're very friendly."

"I've never seen something like that," Rian says, nodding at the dovecote. His tone is so stiff; it couldn't be clearer that he's not a fan, but he absolutely thinks he's tricking us all into thinking he's showing polite interest.

Mom kisses the bird in her hand on the top of its head. Rian can't hide the flash of disgust on his face.

"I have clearly been replaced in my mother's heart," I say.

"Yup," Mom agrees cheerfully.

"So . . . you keep birds?" Rian asks.

"They're noble creatures." Mom holds the pigeon in her hands aloft, as if presenting it to a monarch.

Rian has the tact to say nothing, but his face didn't get the memo.

Mom raises an eyebrow at him, bringing the pigeon back close to her chest. "I'm assuming you're one of those who thinks they're just rats with wings?"

Rian glances at me, but I just shrug. "They do have diseases," he offers weakly.

"Like what?" Mom says, her tone no less sharp despite her smile. "Be specific."

When Rian doesn't produce an answer, Mom smirks. She turns back to the dovecote, replacing the pigeon she'd been holding into its nest and checking over the other birds. "Pigeons have gotten a bad rap historically. You're more likely to be infected with toxoplasma from a kitten than get anything dangerous from one of my babies."

I watch Rian's expression. I wonder if he's got cats on his family's farm. Probably luxury ones, to go with the luxury food they grow. If his Rigel-Earth cats have toxoplasmosis, it's definitely the luxury version of the disease. Toxoplasmosis Elite™.

"It's just not fair," Mom continues. "You know what's the worst of it all?"

"No?" Rian says.

"We domesticated them. Humans, I mean. Pigeons were wild birds, but humans domesticated them. We bred the fear out of them. We turned them into pets. And in the past, we treated them as well as people treat their dogs and cats and any other pet. Better, even. We built palaces for pigeons."

She sweeps her arm grandly at the dovecote, a simple structure made of wood and stone, clean but not ornate.

"Pigeons in the past had a use, though, right?" Rian asks. "They delivered messages. But we don't need that anymore. We have—"

"We have no sense of moral obligation to what we change for our convenience, regardless of what it costs others." Mom speaks with such quiet authority that Rian shuts his mouth mid-sentence.

"Practically every city on Earth has cockroaches, rats, and pigeons," I say. I know Mom's spiel well. "Roaches and rats adapt for survival. But pigeons are everywhere because humans brought them there."

"They love us," Mom says. "A millennium after we tossed them aside like garbage, and they still gather in our cities. They still come up to us, hoping we'll give them kindness. Because our ancestors bred them to trust us."

"And we hate them for it," I add.

Rian looks from me to Mom and back again. "I guess I never thought of it that way."

I join Mom at the dovecote. I'm not a huge fan of birds—their eyes are weird as fuck—but I know Mom's point. And I know why she really keeps the pigeons.

"You know," I tell Mom, "Rian's undersold his expertise to you. He's been doing a lot for the climate-cleaner program."

"The one in all the news feeds?" Mom asks. She turns to Rian, eyes bright. "You're on the team helping to save Earth?"

Rian nods. I'm not sure if he's hesitating now because he's hoping for Mom's approval or because he doesn't want me to talk more.

"Oh, I'm so glad to have met you now," Mom says, beaming at him. "It's like the pigeons."

"Sorry?" Rian asks.

"I keep them because I guess I feel a little responsible. All of these are rescues, ones I've found in New Venice or Valetta, injured or starving. I try to save them because no one else will, and because, well. We have a responsibility, no?"

"To save birds?" Rian asks.

Mom shakes her head. "We have a responsibility to the world we come from. Our ancestors domesticated pigeons and then dumped them when they were no longer useful or beloved. Pigeons can't help that. Can't change the natures bred into and out of them. So, we have a responsibility." She looks from me to him, intently. "Same with Earth and all those people who colonized other worlds. Just because our ancestors polluted Earth to the brink of destroying our whole planet . . . we have a responsibility to it, no? Even the ones who moved away to different worlds. We—humanity— we made a mess, and it's better to clean it than walk away from it."

Rian wasn't expecting bird analogies and human sociology at a rooftop dovecote, but that's what he got. Although I'm not sure Mom's little speech was more for him or me. She's always trying to get to me to think of the *greater good*. Ugh.

Mom contemplates Rian. "I'm guessing from your accent that you're . . ."

"He's from Rigel-Earth," I say.

"Oh, fuck, sorry about that," she tells him.

"I quite like Rigel-Earth," Rian protests.

"Really?" Mom says with the same tone that Rian used when he thought her pigeons were just rats with wings.

"Everyone has their flaws," I mutter to her.

"Yes, but . . . *Rigel-Earth*?" Mom shakes her head.

"Sorry?" Rian says.

"It's okay, dear, you can't help it." Mom closes the dovecote door. "I'll just treat you like one of my pigeons."

"She means that as a compliment," I mutter as we follow her down the steps into the main house, but I don't think Rian believes me.

# 7

We eat dinner on the terrace. There's wine, an occasionally soft coo from the roof, warmth under the solar shield, and crashing waves.

For one meal, we all pretend. We ignore the smells and act like our sun shields are just shirts and all is well. Mom pretends that I'm home visiting, bringing a new boyfriend for her to meet. She keeps feeding Rian like it's her job, and Rian keeps passing the second and third helpings to me because I don't get food this good on the regular. Rian pretends that he's not that important, dodging Mom's questions about his role in the climate-cleaner program.

I pretend like this is normal, and we're going not going to save the world tomorrow.

The sun's well beyond the horizon by the time Rian insists he really is full and needs to go to bed. I set him up in the room Mom keeps for me. It's bland and lacks any decorations, little more than a mattress in a closet.

"It's fine," Rian insists.

"It's because I never lived here, not really," I say, to explain the utter lack of personality in the room. "Mom and Papa split before Papa got sick. And I roomed with friends during university."

And after university, there was only *Glory*. Which, ironically, isn't the type of glory my mother wanted for me, but I'm pretty comfortable with being a disappointment. Not that Mom would call me a disappointment. Maybe I'm just projecting. But damn, it's hard having a saint for a mother. Maybe that's why I'm better off on *Glory* than on Earth. If I'm being honest, nowhere on this planet feels like home the way my ship does. Certainly not here.

I guess the pigeons are more domesticated than me.

"Tomorrow morning—"

"Up early," I confirm. "I've already hired transport to the city. It won't take long."

We'll have to walk part of it. All the streets around Triumph Square are closed to traffic, anyway. I have the route sketched in my head—we'll drop off outside Central Gardens, cut through the public park and the square, then get through security into Fetor Tech.

"It's such a simple plan," Rian starts.

"That's why it'll work. You're used to red tape and layers of clearance. Sometimes, to get something done, all you have to do is walk through the door and do it."

It's kind of amazing the way few people just do the

things they need to do. I don't know how people like Rian convinced humanity that rules should be followed, but it certainly was effective propaganda.

Rian shakes his head. "That door is secured by multiple layers of biometric scans, clearance codes, and ident trackers."

"Which is why I've got you." I punch him lightly in the arm.

He's tense. I am too, but I'm better at hiding it.

"It's going to be fine," I say.

"You absolutely do not know that for certain."

"It's going to be fine, unless we get caught."

"Or fail to change the code."

"That would just fuck up Earth," I point out. As long as we don't get trapped or arrested, we can get away even if the planet is doomed. Still: "No pressure."

"None at all."

I turn to go, then pause at the door. "Hey, Rian?" I ask the dark. I don't have the courage to face him.

"Yeah?"

"When this is all over—all of it, I mean. Penthouse suite in the most expensive hotel in the city, you and me and buckets of chocolate-covered strawberries?"

He's silent for a long time. So long that I almost walk away.

Then I hear his deep chuckle. "Yeah. I'll bring some more peaches, too."

I whirl around, eyes alight. "Okay, actually, if you bring

me some of those peaches, you don't even need to bring yourself; I can have that moment without you."

His eyes are liquid and feral. "Oh, no," he says, both a promise and a threat. "I absolutely intend to be there." A heartbeat. "And it'll be more than a moment."

My body does all those things I've been trying to tell it not to do all week. We're both lying, still acting like this is a future we can have. It's a game, one we'll lose even if we win, and we know it.

But it's worth the fantasy. For tonight, anyway.

"All I have to do is save the world tomorrow, and I get you and peaches and all night in a penthouse suite?" I ask. "I may need that in writing."

His voice is pitched low. "I keep my promises, Ada."

Fuck me sideways, I know he does.

I need a cold shower, but instead, I have to face my mother. I find her on the roof, illuminated only by a light near the door and the full moon. It's weird to think that I was kicking up my heels on the lunar station just a little bit ago.

"He in bed?" Mom asks. She drank half a bottle of wine by herself, but her voice is sharp and clear.

"He's in the bedroom, but . . ." *But we need to be careful what we say.*

"Got it." *He could come up here and spy on us, or he could have dropped a listening device.*

"How are you feeling about tomorrow?" Mom asks.

"Confident."

Mom smirks at that. She knows me well.

Just as she knows the plan. The *real* one.

I drop a hand to my belly. "Although a little queasy. Planetary gravity always fucks me over." The only thing worse than planning a high-stakes heist with your enemy? Doing it while on your period, which has come with a hell of a punch, straight to the uterus.

"Ugh, sorry," Mom says. "Do you need anything?"

"I took some meds. And I'm drinking all the coffee tomorrow. All of it." Caffeine helps. And it's hard to get beans in space. It was just crummy timing and inaccessible meds while I was in the black that led to this.

I touch my ear, the one unadorned. Mom's eyes follow me.

"You lost an earring," she says.

"I know. At the gala." I know she knows what I mean: *That part of the mission was a success.*

Mom leans over and looks at my other earring.

The pair are a matching set, but they're far, far more than they appear. I wore them to the gala on purpose.

Kidnapping Rian was only one goal, after all. And these high-tech earrings are pretty nifty. The one I still have hasn't been used yet. The other one—the one I "lost" at the gala—is a code scanner. Tiny, wireless, put it next to any computer using basic coding, and it scans the data, recording it for analysis later.

"How was the gala?" Mom asks.

"It went well, I hope." *We'll find out how well after tomorrow.*

Mom nods. Her face is grave, her shoulders tight.

"Why did you want me to come visit, Mom?" I ask softly. What we both know I mean is: *Your cover is going to get blown now. Why did you force my hand to get me here?*

I *might* have been able to distract Rian from how I have a residency claim to Malta through my mother. He might have glossed over the fact that he didn't find much information about her in her official records. I could have done things to help facilitate a ploy big enough to pull his razor eyes away from my mother and her tower full of birds.

It's too late now.

That's why I couldn't let him get a hotel—why I have to control who he sees and communicates with at least until tomorrow and the mission is done. It's not just that he could call in backup. One deep dive into my mother's identity, and he will notice that the holes in her record have been sliced out with surgical precision.

By me.

Mom still hasn't answered my question. "We didn't have

to come here," I say gently. "We could have pinged the locator and then gone to a hotel or back to my ship."

"I'm aware," she says curtly.

"You've been here a long time." *Are you going to have to leave now?*

"I'm aware of that, too." *Maybe. Probably.*

She looks a little sadly at the dovecote. Everything we say, everything we do—it has double meaning. Just in case someone else is listening.

Just in case it's Rian.

I've brought the enemy into my mother's home.

But in my defense, she invited him.

"You're aware . . ." I say slowly. "But I'm missing something."

One curt nod.

Fuck.

I'm missing something. There's an angle here I'm not seeing.

"I got a message from the Moon," Mom says.

*I* didn't send a message to her from the station while *Glory* was waiting for landing sequences and clearance codes.

*Rian* sent a message. Not to her, obviously.

But a message she intercepted or was forwarded. Perhaps from our mutual contact, Phoebe, the double agent on Rian's team who's only our friend as long as we share a goal. More likely, this is one of Mom's contacts, someone loyal to her.

She has a *lot* of friends.

Few people know the full extent of my mother's network. Obscurity helps.

I feel a pang of sympathy for Rian when he inevitably figures all this out. He's had his targets locked on to me so intensely that he didn't even realize there was a bigger fish in my shadow. All those times he's pressed me for who I worked for. It's true; I take the jobs that come. But since Rian's been watching me, my work has mostly come from one source.

All along, my client was my mother.

All along, my mother was Jane Irwin.

My mother was working secretly to facilitate change on Earth before my father even got sick. She used an older family name for a small level of anonymity, not knowing how quickly it would latch on. It started as an underground network to redistribute medicine to people who, like Papa, got sick and couldn't afford treatment. But options were limited, and there was no black market for the meds that *really* worked. Papa's death from climate sickness—a death that could have been wholly prevented, had people like Fetor not been so adamant about seeing profits from the treatments and vaccines—broke something inside of both of us.

For me, every fuck I ever had to give was drained from my body.

But Mom couldn't save Papa. So, she decided to save Earth instead.

I know it disappoints her, the way I won't join her rebellion, the way I demand payment even when I work for her. But I also know that she, more than any other human in the galaxy, understands why I am the way I am.

And she loves me anyway.

Which means, even when I don't want to get involved, for her, I will.

For her, I'll save the world.

I'll just also make sure I get paid—with bonuses—along the way.

"It's almost time for bed," Mom says. She leans in for a hug, and when her lips are centimeters from my ear, she whispers, "He's going to betray you."

I hold her tight. It really has been too long.

"I know," I whisper back.

I've known since he came back with blue puff cubes in one hand and a guilty look all over his face. Not the exacts of the message he sent, of course, but I knew he had sent a message.

I had told him it was a risk for me to let him out of my sight on the station.

I lied, obviously.

Because he had never been out of my sight.

And the risk? It was never mine.

*Fucking hell,* I think, my arms still wrapped around my mother's slender shoulders, thinner than the last time we saw each other in person.

I let him go because I wanted to see if, maybe, he wouldn't do the thing he did.

I wanted to see if, given the opportunity, he wouldn't betray me.

But he did.

"I'm working on something," Mom says. "For you."

"Can I know the details?"

She shakes her head. She's still working on the plan to get me out of Rian's clutches, but it's not solid yet.

"Any chance I'll see you when this is all done?" I ask, finally pulling out of my mom's embrace.

Her smile is hard. Worried.

"I hope so," she says, doubt evident. She pauses. "Ada? I am so, *so* proud of you."

I give her a flat look. "You know I'm only in this for fun and profit."

"Still." Mom tucks a stray lock of hair behind my ear. She hates the way I have it cut; I cut it this way partly because she hates it so much. It's how we work.

If she opens the door, I want to stay. If she closes it, I want to go. I define myself as a reaction to her definitions.

"How early are you leaving tomorrow?" Mom asks.

"Very." I tell her the time I have set on my alarm.

"I have a present for you before you go."

Ah, there it is. The reason why she sent a message to Bruna to relay to me, the reason why she made sure she was here and insisted that we stay when I arrived.

She wants to help me escape the trap Rian has laid for me.

I give her a look, and she shrugs. She doesn't know the specifics of how Rian will betray me.

She only knows he will.

*He's going to betray me.* I knew it was a possibility from the start. But a part of me had believed in penthouse suites and luxury peaches and more than a night. More than a night.

He'll wait, of course, for the mission to be a success. He knows that I'm the linchpin in reprogramming the nano-bots, so he'll make sure I can do the job. But after? That's when he'll strike.

A job isn't finished when the last piece of the puzzle falls into place.

A job is only finished after the getaway.

# 8

We're all up before the sun the next morning.

Rian and I sit at the table in the main room; there's more space here than in the cramped personal living area one floor down. Rian's jazzed up the standard-issue clothes I got for him with his coat from the gala, the informal balancing out the ultra-formal in a look that I could see some feeds picking up as a new trend, especially paired with the easy way Rian wears it all. My outfit is simple enough, all skintight black, and that gives enough of an air of elegance that will allow me to pass through Fetor Tech unnoticed. I catch Rian appreciating the way the slinky material clings to my body. I wonder if he's realized loose clothing is a liability, something easily grabbed.

Mom bustles around, ostensibly giving us food and filling my coffee cup as soon as I take a sip. But there's a method to her movements, purpose in every trip downstairs. While Rian spent the night in "my" bedroom, I slept in my mother's bed . . . but she wasn't there all night. There were a lot of moving parts to pin down for her operation.

Rian and I are planning a heist that requires precise timing and luck; Mom's planning something else just as precarious. It's strange to share a table with so many secrets.

When Mom goes up to feed the birds, I pull out a thin sheet of plastic speckled with tiny clear stickers: two round ones and two rectangles.

I peel off one circular sticker and press it into the smooth skin behind my left ear, the one without an earring. There's a little bead in the center of the sticker, and I push it hard against my skull. I take one rectangular sticker and smooth it down just below the collar of my shirt, in the hollow space above my clavicle, under my throat.

When I pass him the plastic sheet, Rian does the same.

Bone-conducting hearing devices behind our ears, subvocal transmitters at our throats. Crude technology, but it works.

*Testing*, I say without opening my lips or moving my jaw. It's barely a hum; if we weren't in a silent, empty room, even I wouldn't be able to hear the sound.

A moment later, the robotic voice translating Rian's subvocal reply vibrates in my bone-conducting audio transmitter: *Received*.

Subvocal isn't great for detailed messages; the artificial intelligence built into the chip relies on context and guesses to form complicated sentences, but for a few words— especially when we need to give each other warnings—this will work well.

"You have all you need?" Rian asks.

I touch my right ear and the silver stud earring. My other earring, the one I left at the gala, was a code scanner, receiving whatever code I needed.

This one is the opposite: it replaces code.

I wrote the program myself, and I spent the past week in the portal on the voyage from Rigel-Earth to here checking and rechecking it. I built the code like a virus—all I have to do is upload it into the nanobot program, and it will overwrite the malware Strom Fetor had added in.

"I'll need an hour," I remind Rian.

He scowls. "I'll buy you all the time I can."

An hour is going to be tight for the plan to work. "I can't help how long it takes for code to get uploaded. It's not instantaneous."

"I know," he grumbles. He's a nervous ball of energy, fiddling with the plastic backing of the comm stickers.

I reach over and touch his hand. He looks up, eyes locking on mine.

"It's going to be fine," I say.

He smiles ruefully. "You're a good liar."

"I am."

"At least one of us has confidence."

"Before you go," Mom calls from the stairs, announcing her presence. She bursts through the door, a box in her hands.

"What's that?" I ask.

Mom shrugs, setting it down on the table in front of me. "I have no idea. You told me weeks ago you were having a package delivered here; don't you remember?"

If only Rian knew I learned how to lie from my mother. Whatever is in this box must be the reason why she made sure Bruna sent me here and insisted on being here when Rian and I arrived.

I brush aside the pigeon feather stuck to the box. The gray feather loops and swirls as it drifts down, and I glance at Mom, who's staring at me. Hard. That feather was part of the message.

I rip into the package, withdrawing . . .

"A sun shield?" Rian asks. "Why did you buy a new one?"

Clever, clever Mother. "This is not just any sun shield," I say.

Mom heads downstairs to make another pot of coffee. And give me a chance to pretend to Rian like I planned for this all along.

"Hold your scanner up to it," I say as I take my shirt off, slip the sun shield over my head, and smooth it against my body. The paper-thin material blends into my skin, almost unnoticeable—and anyone who did notice it would think nothing of it, given our location. I pull my shirt back on over it. Only the hood dangling over the collar behind my neck stands out, but my hair covers most of that.

Rian lifts his cuff up, looking at me through the recorder lens built into it. I pull the hood over my hair, obscuring part of my face.

"Smart," Rian says in an appreciative tone.

All sun shields block radiation from contributing to skin cancer or climate sickness. This one also blocks camera lenses. It's woven with tiny reflective threads from Gliese-Earth that cast light flares and sparkles, making it hard to capture a clean shot, especially one that could be used for identification. The brighter the area, the worse the image captured.

And Fetor Tech's headquarters are *very* bright.

"But . . ." Rian's voice trails off.

"What?" I demand.

"Nothing. But. Just . . ."

*"What?"*

"There's going to be a record. I'll have to check you in as a guest. When we get into the nanobot programming room, the only way that works is if I use all my credentials to open the door. Fetor is going to know it's us. Why even bother with a disguise like that?"

Once I reprogram the nanobots, there's no hiding Rian's involvement. But there's also nothing Fetor will be able to do about it—the nanobots themselves will be given the exact programming that they were always supposed to have, the programming that was approved. *Fetor* violated those terms by reprogramming them to fail in a system that would benefit him.

Once again, nothing I'm doing is *technically* illegal. Except for the parts that are, but Fetor won't be able to prosecute me, because then it would expose what he did to everyone in the galaxy, and he won't risk that.

"It's not a perfect disguise, but it's another layer of protection once I'm inside," I say. "No one will blink twice at a sun shield. But the security drones won't get a read on me, and any cams recording will get corrupted."

The drones might trigger a higher level of security if they can't get a facial scan, of course, but probably not. Or, hopefully, at least not within the hour I need to be inside the building. Our plan hinges on timing and calculated risks, and this certainly can't hurt. Rian seems to agree; he doesn't question it further.

I glance at the feather that dropped on the floor when I opened the box.

By the time we should depart, I'm jittery from caffeine and sick to my stomach from nerves, even if I don't show them. Also, biology is being a bitch, but other than that and the concept that what we're doing in the next few hours may doom or save Earth, to say nothing of my own personal prospects, everything's fine.

Just fine.

We go by boat. Friend-of-a-friend network leaves no

records; it's Bruna's cousin who picks us up and takes us around the south end of Gozo to the massive bridge that connects the two big islands together, forming the city of New Venice.

We're dropped off at a platform that connects to the lifts that rise up from the sea level all the way to the bridge city atop us. It's early, but locals crowd the area, and it'll be a while before we can go up. Rian frowns—nerves, I think, or he's still mad we didn't get a nearer hotel.

Luzzu boats huddle under the bridge, waiting for tourists to summon them for a scenic waterway ride through sanitized routes. It's early enough that the workers and their families are sleeping in the boats, under dark cloths that afford them a little privacy.

I glance at Rian.

I don't think he sees that there are people under the blankets. His eyes glide over the scene, barely taking in the colorfully painted boats, much less what's in their shadows. His gaze lingers on the underside of the massive city-bridge, illuminated with sparkling lights for the tourists. I wonder if he's looking for rust. If he sees that an entire city resting atop a massive manmade structure connecting two islands isn't exactly the safest design in the world. I wonder if he's thinking it'll fall one day, and if he's concerned first with the people who live in the huge buildings atop the bridge or the ones who live in the boats beneath it.

We're both looking for problems, but we're looking in the opposite direction.

Rian turns and catches me staring at him. "What?"

I pat his cheek. "You have keen eyes, but there's a lot you don't see."

He catches my hand, holds it next to his skin, warm and flush. "I see more than you think I do."

Clear hazel, sharp as broken glass and honed blades.

*He's going to betray you.*

My mother's voice, shattering the moment.

But I don't take a step back.

And neither does he.

And when I tip up on my toes on the shaky platform, he meets me halfway.

*He's going to betray you.*

I know.

I always knew.

When his arms go to my waist, I know he's feeling for more than my skin—he's looking for weapons or for devices I can use against him. My hand presses against his hard chest, and I note the way his heart beats but also the hard edges of a data recorder in his pocket, something that may be able to connect to a communication network.

When we kiss, we both keep our eyes open.

# 9

"Ready to save the world?" he asks, his voice husky.

"Don't be dramatic; this is just a normal Monday."

We push through the crowds to the lift. It deposits us in the warm, early morning light of a sunrise, the orange-red glow reflected off the skyscrapers towering over the city.

This lift brings us right to the gates of Central Gardens. At the corner, across the street, we pass a mental spa with bright lights, advertising its services. All the shops are just starting to open up, smells of rich food wafting out, enticing me.

"Not yet," Rian says, grabbing my elbow and steering me toward the park.

"Just a little—"

"Focus." His voice is stern enough that I'm distracted from the buttery, sweet smell of fresh pastries blended with the savory scents of spiced sausages. It's *decadent.* If these people knew just how hard it is to hide the taste of goopy-yet-nutrient-dense recycler worm waste with hot sauce, they'd spend all their cash on honey rings and froġa tat-tarja and pastizzi.

Central Gardens is a large park, a rare spot of green open to all. The meandering paths are carefully maintained and structured to encourage you to take your time, but we go at a fast clip. At least until we see the enormous floating screens.

"What are these?" I ask, peering up at the nearest one. It's larger than a window, round, and illuminated with a video of some other city, streets crowded. From the background, I'd guess maybe Centauri-Earth.

"Communication Viewing Rings," Rian says. "Not my department, but I helped approve the installation."

I keep walking, heading to the next floating screen. A different image in this one—it shows a city in China. The next one is Rigel-Earth—I can tell just from the way the people are dressed. Through it I see a woman looking at her reflection in a shop window. It reminds me, weirdly, of the dusty shops we passed in Xlendi, the way I couldn't have caught my reflection if I'd tried.

"The climate-cleaner project is big," Rian reminds me. "The entire galaxy is watching. The CVRs are supposed to promote inclusivity and goodwill." He sounds like he's reciting information from a press release. For all I know, he is.

A boy from Rigel-Earth a little younger than us stops, peering through the video. He touches his arm and frowns, which makes me look at my own arms. I'm guessing the sun shield's flare threads are making it hard for him to accurately see me; he can tell I'm there but can't spot the details. There's no sound from the view ring, just visual.

"This is a live feed?" I ask.

"As close to live as possible." Rian points beyond the trees, where the top of Fetor Towers is visible. "It helps to be boosted by the comm network hub."

"I bet," I mumble. The boy from Rigel-Earth in the screen scowls at me, probably shocked to have a window into such a disadvantaged planet as mine. I pull up my sleeve and flip him off.

"Ada!" Rian protests. "Inclusivity and goodwill!"

The boy in the screen returns my rude gesture. For a moment, we both stare at each other, separated by lightyears and worlds away. Then a smile twitches at my lips, visible since I don't have my hood up, and the boy on the other side of the galaxy snorts in silent laughter.

"Would you look at that," I say, heading back down the path and past even more floating screens. "There's one decent person on the entire planet of Rigel-Earth, and I happened to catch him in your little inclusivity project."

"One?" Rian asks.

"Apparently." I pull my hood up; it's too easy to forget about sun protection in the cool, early morning, but radiation doesn't care about temperature.

The park spills out into a stone expanse. There are more

of the view rings all around Triumph Square, as well as more people. Food carts are already strategically positioned throughout the courtyard, and vendors mill about. There's always a crowd at Triumph Square, but it's clear that people expect this to be a big celebration, gathering hours before the scheduled launch.

Eight . . . nine . . . more than a dozen of the people here could be Rian's. I catch eyes that follow us, stiff postures. I could be wrong.

*He's going to betray you.*

I also spot at least ten uniformed officers. Big crowds, big security.

"Look." Rian points to the front of Fetor Tech. The building holds the prime real estate at the side of the square opposite Central Gardens.

An *enormous* display illuminates holographic numbers that encompass the entire front of the building. As I watch, the numbers melt, counting down by the minute. It's supposed to be a kickoff to the celebration of the launch of the climate-cleaner nanobots, but I can't help but feel like this is a personal taunting, reminding Rian and me of how little time we have to do what needs to be done.

"It's fine," I mumble, grabbing his hand and dragging him toward Fetor Tech. A tight timeline is a complication but a calculated one.

While in the portal pathway between the gala on Rigel-

Earth and the nanobot release here, today, Rian and I went over every schematic of Fetor Tech, combining it with his personal knowledge of the building. Fetor Tech has some of the best and latest technological security systems, but it's still a huge building where lots of workers and guests need to come and go.

It's not as big as some buildings, though, which helps. Because the city of New Venice is built on top of a bridge, there are limits to the size of the skyscrapers. Fetor Tech is the tallest building in the entirety of Malta, but it's less than fifty stories high, although topped with a pretty tall communications tower. Impressive, but I do like to think that Strom Fetor is personally affronted by the size limitations of his building.

Regardless, step one: get inside.

This is the easy part. Rian already has full clearance to be anywhere in the building. It takes a solid fifteen minutes for the guard in the lobby to deign to register me as Rian's guest, and despite the way it makes my stomach surge, I have my ident scanned and a proper record created of my entry, and I do it with a smile as if this were all casual.

"She's allowed into the viewing room on floor forty-two," the guard says, bored.

"I have to stop by the main office and the server room first," Rian says. He's laying the path now so there's no question when he accesses those rooms—with me—later.

"Then she has to wait on floor forty-two for you," the guard says, his attention more focused.

"I know."

Something about his tone makes the guard narrow his gaze at Rian. "Your scans are tracked," he says. "She physically will *not* be allowed into the server room or any of the higher floors, and if you try to have her jump the gate with you, I *will* be alerted."

"I *know*," Rian says.

I play a game on my cuff, pretending I'm bored senseless by this all.

Finally, the guard says, "Take the last elevator on the left."

When we're in the lift, Rian has to scan his fingerprint before he even pushes the button for the floor we need. Numbers zip by on the display as we rise, and the metal tube gives way to glass, showing the ever-increasing crowd at Triumph Square below.

"You really don't interact with people well."

"That guard had a chip on his shoulder!" Rian protests.

I shrug. "I *know*," I say, an exact imitation of his petulant voice.

Rian rolls his eyes. "At least Fetor cares more about tech than people."

"No guards on the forty-second floor?"

"A few. We can't get slack."

"I never do." Besides, we've been over this before. Fetor's love of technology—and his overbearing need to show off that love—means that we have to trick machines more than people now that we've cleared the first hurdle.

It definitely works in my favor that Fetor's so pretentious that he loves artificial intelligence more than human. Then again, I suspect that *artificial* is the only sort of intelligence that can put up with the asshole.

The elevator deposits us in a big room being set up by caterers with towers of champagne and platters of nibbles.

"No," Rian says, gripping my elbow and steering me away.

"But!" My body drifts toward a table where workers are setting up a truly elaborate series of interlocking trays, each one loaded down with a different delectable goodie.

*"No,"* Rian says again, more emphatically.

Fine. I can wait. The caterers aren't even done setting up yet. I can wait. And then I'm going to eat everything in sight, and I'll punch Rian in the throat if he tries to stop me.

Rian waves at a few people he clearly recognizes from his time spent in this building, making small talk. We still have hours until launch, and none of the guests of honor are here, but I doubt much work is going to happen in this building today. It's corporate party time. People are milling about, finding excuses to come out and watch the caterers set up rather than sit at their desks. Which is a pain in the ass, because it would be great if everyone could just leave. I wonder if I could get away with pulling a fire alarm.

Probably not.

Would be fun, though.

On the far side of the open area I can see golden elevator doors. This is not the same lift that Rian and I used to get to this floor, silver and glass. At least a dozen security guards stand in front of the velvet-rope barrier separating this elevator from the rest of the public.

I know what this is because Rian told me already. The private elevator that Strom Fetor and his inner circle use. If the elevator to get to this floor required clearing a single security guard and then Rian scanning his fingerprint before pushing the button, the golden elevator is going to be even worse.

"I can't wait to go up there," a man says, sidling up to us. Rian nods at him, but before he can introduce us, the man holds out his hand and gives me his name: Haoyu Long. "I've been working here a decade, and I've never been up to the real office."

"Oh, you should have just done what I did," I say, looping my arm through Rian's. "Sleep with someone with an invite."

Haoyu laughs, then sobers, considering.

"Anyway," Rian says awkwardly, "I'm going to introduce Ada around before I have to go into my office for a bit."

I wave at Haoyu as Rian pulls me toward a nearby woman who says her name is Dante. I'm not sure if that's her given or her family name, but then I get distracted by the way Rian introduces me: "My date, Ada." Has a nice ring to it.

The woman's eyes widen a little in surprise, but she embraces me warmly.

"We wondered if he'd bring someone," she says, winking. "It's rare enough to get to visit the boss's office, but only a handful were given guest invites."

Then she turns to Rian. "Bev is going to be so disappointed!"

"Bev?" I ask, because it's painfully obvious that Rian doesn't want to continue the conversation.

"Bev's not exactly been subtle about—" Dante starts.

"I really need to talk to Ngabo," Rian says, cutting her off. "I should introduce Ada to him. Then I have to make a quick stop in my office."

"I wanna hear about Bev and all the people trying to date you!" I protest as Rian drags me off to meet Ngabo Gatwa, a communications director getting coffee on the other side of the room.

Soon after I shake hands with Ngabo, Rian tells me has to introduce me to someone named Melissa Nguyen, whose office is down the hall. We make our way through handshakes and small talk until we reach a corner. Rian strides confidently down the interior hallway, most of the doors shut and the lights off. Everyone's finding excuses to not be doing their jobs. I'm glad I didn't pull the fire alarm; this area is deserted enough.

"So, I'm your date?" I say coyly as we go farther and farther from the pleasantly smiling people who have no idea what we're doing.

Rian rolls his eyes.

"Should I be worried about this Bev person?" I add.

"No." Rian grits the word out through clenched teeth.

"I could fight her for your affection."

"That is unnecessary."

"Because you adore me and cannot even contemplate being with someone else?" I ask, beaming and putting a literal skip in my step.

"Because— Ugh." Rian opens a door, motioning for me to hurry inside.

On the other side of the door is a plain stairwell.

"One flight up," I say, my tone low but serious. Rian nods and shuts the door in my face.

I sprint to the steps.

Rian is going to use his clearance to go up one more level—he was given an office on the floor below Fetor's. That's our loophole. He's spent all this time ensuring that we're seen and friendly and peppering in reminders that he has to go into his office. Sometimes, the best way to hide is to announce to everyone exactly where you plan to be.

The security guard downstairs got me clearance to the floor where the reception is—all the menial workers who *actually* do the work, even if Fetor's going to get all the credit. The employees get snacks and a chance to go up the golden elevators for all their hard labor, and I guess they think that's enough.

Either way, I've got to get up there before everyone else.

The golden elevator? Out of the question. Right now, as I bound up the steps in this emergency stairwell, Rian is showing his badge to the security guards, and then he has an eye scan and another fingerprint press before he can go up to his own office. But he's going to walk right past his office and instead let me in through the stairwell door.

I rush up the steps. There are cam drones here in the emergency stairwell, but when they buzz by, I pin myself to the wall, trusting that my altered sun shield is enough to register as a weird flare, not even a person. They don't even pause when they pass me.

Tech can be easier to fool than people.

At least I hope so. I'm definitely gambling a lot on that theory.

# UNITED GALACTIC SYSTEM

**MEMO**

**To:** Rian White
**From:** Phoebe Brücke
**Re:** Climate-Cleaner Launch

Dear Sir:

I am uncertain if you will receive this prior to accessing reliable communication networks. Please be advised that all security measures have been enacted to your recommendation. Agents are in position to move in at your signal.

One additional note: our officers have been monitoring all known networks of the various organizations that we suspect A█ L█████ has been a part of, particularly the organization referenced in-house as Green Rogue, under the presumed leadership of an agent code-named Jane Irwin. There has been *zero* communication in regards to the climate-cleaner launch from that group, with no pings on the network within the region.

It is unknown if A█ L█████ is no longer working for that organization, never worked for that organization, or if our network monitoring has been detected and alternative means of communication are being used.

Should it come to light that Green Rogue is using an alternative form of communication, we may be at a disadvantage. It seems likely that this—a major conservation effort on Sol-Earth—would have attracted their attention, so the lack of buzz on the comms has been disconcerting.

In short, I fear we are missing something important.

# 10

Floor forty-two is going to get more and more crowded as the next few hours go by. It's just the employees now, taking advantage of the celebrations to avoid work for today and scarf as much catered food as they can before the media shows up.

I can't believe I walked away before the tower of platters was set up. What the fuck was I thinking?

Right, save the world first. Food after.

Still, it's almost with reluctance that I reach the stairwell door labeled FORTY-THREE. There is no handle here, and it's locked from the other side. It's definitely a weak spot, though, as evidenced by the way Rian opens it up for me from the inside. *He* had to go through clearance, but more eyes are on Fetor's personal office, not this one. I mean, it's also not the only level of security, but still.

We head to the server room where the nanobots are stored and developed. It's climate-controlled and on a private network relay. The building is pretty much square, and on this floor, the server room takes up the entire middle, with offices lining the outside. I try not to think about how that means all the food is right under all the nanobots.

"This feels too easy," Rian mumbles.

"This is a government-funded project built by a private company," I say. "And that private company is run by a dumbass who lucked into wealth and power."

He frowns, and when he glances at me, I'm pretty sure he can see that I agree with him, despite my bravado. We're both waiting for the other shoe to drop.

We stop outside the server room. Getting on this floor required a loophole. Getting through this door? It's going to take a little more luck.

Rian stands in front of a small step beside the door, his face pressed against a scanner built into the wall, doing a retinal scan as well as basic facial recognition. At the same time, he has his left palm on a different glass pane, a red light scanning his entire handprint. When he steps back, a PIN pad pops out, and he punches in a twelve-digit alphanumeric code.

The door slides open.

"Ready?" Rian asks.

I adjust my sun shield.

"As I'll ever be." I step through the door.

It closes automatically behind me.

*In,* I say, using the subvocal transmitters.

Rian says something in reply, but then another voice fills the room, computerized. "Visual sensors disrupted."

Yeah, flare threads in a sun shield will do that.

*You didn't tell me there was more security* in *the room,* I tell Rian with the subvocal transmitter.

*I didn't know there was.*

"Inconclusive results," the robotic voice says. "Please remove any material that blocks visual input."

"Yeah, that's not happening."

On either side of me in this narrow entryway are two lenses, the rounded glass moving as the red-light sensors rove over my body. The door registers who's logging in, then the person who enters the room is scanned to make sure the biometric scans and PIN-pad key match the person who steps inside.

The system is designed to stop people from doing exactly what Rian and I are trying to do.

*Shit.*

"Please stand still; rescanning," the computer says.

*There's a fucking body scanner in here,* I say, stepping out of the entry and away from the scanners.

"You are required to rescan," the computer says.

*I didn't know that,* Rian says.

Of course he wouldn't. The scans on his body have always matched the biometrics and PIN-pad key. When *he* walks through the door, the computer is silent and doesn't protest.

The only saving grace right now is the sun shield with flare threads. It's enough to throw off the system and put it into an error rather than straight to blaring alarms.

"You are required to rescan," the computer says as I sprint down the corridor to where Rian said the nanobots would be stored. I take out my earring; all I have to do is slide the metal post into the input port, and the code will go from the stud into the nanobot reprogrammer.

"You have fourteen minutes, thirty-two seconds to rescan before system alerts security."

*Fuck, fuck, fuck,* I think. Except I must have done it subvocally, because Rian answers.

*Is everything okay?*

*No,* I snap back, skidding around a corner. *We have less than fifteen before the system locks me in and alerts all the guards to come drag me away.*

*What? Why?*

"Because it has a fucking body scanner inside!" I say out loud. The subvocal transmitter won't pick that up, so I have to repeat it in an impatient hum as I slam toward the back of the room, frantically looking over the shelves.

*I can override the system and cancel the lockdown,* Rian says.

*Really?* I ask.

*I think? Maybe?*

Cool, cool, that eases my mind. Love a man with confidence.

This room holds more than just Fetor's nanobot program. It's a server room for most of Fetor Tech's processes, and it's cluttered with enticingly interesting prototypes I want to play with.

"Twelve minutes to system lockdown," the computer voice announces cheerily.

Right, focus.

Nanobots are tiny. Microscopically tiny. The climate-cleaner program is designed to send enough bots out into the water system of Earth that eventually, the pollutants are stripped from the oceans and the atmosphere. It's designed to change the entire water cycle of Earth.

But the bots themselves are small enough to fit inside a shoebox.

*I can't override the system while you're inside,* Rian says. *How much time do you have left?*

*Maybe ten minutes,* I say, moments before the computer voice confirms.

*Can you get it done and get out by then? I can shut it down once you're back outside.*

Fuck me, this is going to cut everything super close.

*I told you before,* I say subvocally. *I need an hour, minimum.*

*Get out as soon as you can, and we can re-assess. There has to be something we can do.*

Rian's going to break my heart with all the hope he crams into those words. All the impossible, foolish hope.

The back wall of this room is a massive supercomputer, but I see the system Rian told me about, the nanobot programmer. I see the input port. Theoretically, all I have to do is put my earring post into the port.

"Eight minutes to system lockdown," the computer voice announces.

*Rian, we have a big fucking problem,* I say.

*Just get out. I can shut down the lockdown system when you're out. We'll figure it out.*

*No,* I say, fiddling with my earring. *Something far, far worse.*

*What can be worse than getting caught and locked in?*

I take a deep breath, looking over the wall, the shelves, everything stored here. There are so many toys I could play with. So much chaos I could cause.

So much profit to be had.

I turn on my heel and sprint back.

The computer tells me I still have four minutes before lockdown by the time I slam my fist into the control to open the door.

Rian reaches through the doorway, grabbing my arm and yanking me back into the corridor. The door zips shut once I'm through, and Rian punches a series of codes into the PIN pad, scans his face again, and then taps out another code.

From here, I cannot hear the computerized voice counting down, but one look on Rian's relieved face informs me that he got that part shut down. No alarm is going to go off. Human security isn't coming.

"Can you tell me what to do? I can go in, get all scanned, and set up the code thing to reprogram the bots . . ." Rian's voice trails off as he takes in my defeated expression. "The problem's bigger than that."

"Yup."

His whole body deflates. "What is it?"

I bite my lip.

"Tell me I can go in for you and reprogram the bots," Rian pleads.

"I would tell you that," I say, "if the nanobots had been in the room."

# 11

The color drains from Rian's face. "They moved the bots?" When I don't answer, he curses. "They moved the fucking bots."

Makes sense. We are cutting it this close to launch so that the climate cleaners are released before anyone notices we reverted the code to the originally approved design. But this close to launch means that they can be moved earlier than scheduled, and there's not a single fucking thing we can do about it without tipping our hand.

"Where would they be moved to?" I demand, gripping Rian's arms, noting the tight muscles under his sleeves. I have to get him to refocus, and fast.

Rian shakes his head. "I went over every plan. They were not supposed to be moved yet."

"Well, the plan's changed." I dip my head, forcing him to make eye contact. "Where could they be?"

"They're launching from the communications tower," Rian says. "Rooftop."

*Fan-fucking-tastic.*

The thing is: it's not like you just open Pandora's box of nanobots and they fly up like accommodating little drones. No, the bots have to be actively launched. From a computer terminal—one that I can hack. So even if I have to change location last-minute, it's not too late.

"Can you get me there?" I demand.

Rian's mouth is tight. He's not the kind of man to just answer first and think it through later. I know in his mind, he's running through every possible path this deviation has created. Getting into the communications room will mean less security to clear than in the server room but more possible witnesses. Human ones who won't be distracted by my sun shield, who won't give me a fifteen-minute grace period to override their suspicions.

While all the workers in the climate-cleaner program are probably already digging in to the caterers' trays, there will be workers in the communication tower not invited to the party. We have to get past them . . . somehow.

"I think we can do it," he says finally.

So many emotions flicker over his face—most of them rooted in panic—that I'm a little worried the man's going to flop over here on the floor.

He takes a deep, shaky breath.

"I don't like this either, but—" I start.

"We have to," he finishes. Rian's eyes meet mine, and

even if I can still see the unease in them, there's determination there, too.

"One goal," I remind him gently.

Full speed until we get it.

We take off running. Everyone in the building is either one floor below us, taking advantage of all the delicious food, or one floor up, with Fetor's elite. Not everyone's getting an invite up the golden elevator.

But the communications office is a big glass room built atop the roof, with a launch zone and antennas sticking up over it. Like old-school airport traffic-control rooms, that office never closes. There *will* be workers there.

But that's the thing. They'll be working. Everyone in that room has a job to do. They'll be focused on that.

I hope.

"We just have to act like we belong," I say for myself as much as Rian. "People don't question authority."

Rian shoots me a withering look as he scans his fingerprint on the elevator-call button. "All you do is question authority."

"Yeah, but most people aren't like me."

"Thankfully," he mutters. I choose to ignore that.

Instead, I focus on everything I know about the communications room at Fetor Tech while we wait for the elevator.

This is *the* communication hub for the entire galactic

system, so of course I've researched this before. The communication office is the foundational network for the portal system. It never goes down. It never fails—despite being associated with Strom Fetor. It's one of those things in society, like the power grid, the healthcare system, or travel regulations, that if it goes down, all of society is impacted. Although run by the private Fetor Tech company, it's heavily monitored and works hand-in-hand with the government, which uses the comm system developed into the portal rings for all intergalactic communication.

"Nervous?" Rian asks as a bell announces the arrival of the lift.

I force my hands to still. I had been practicing the movements I need for the next play, but I should have known he'd notice.

"Never." I shoot him a grin.

"Yeah, same." He jabs the button for the roof after holding the door for me to go inside first.

We don't talk. A million random different thoughts—half of them questions about when the food will be available—boil up to my teeth, but I keep my mouth closed.

*Focus.*

The doors slide open.

Rian steps out first.

We're in a glass-covered walkway, and while the floor

beneath our feet is covered in lush carpet, beyond the clear tube there's just cement and the rest of the roof. The path takes us directly to a large building that takes up about a quarter of the space, on the eastern side, closest to Triumph Square. The rest of the roof is littered with poles and towers; when I crane my neck up, I can almost see the tips of the various satellites and receivers the communication system uses.

"Focus," Rian says, grabbing my arm and dragging me toward the offices. At the door, he has to do another security check—PIN pad, face and hand scans—but when the doors glide open, I just step in with him, basically cramming through the till. It's inelegant but effective.

We're in.

For one breathless moment, I wait to see if there's a secondary scan to stop us from doing just this. But no computerized voice pipes up. None of the workers even glance our way. I was right. This is a place of work, and everyone's too focused on their own high-stakes job to notice anyone else's arrival.

Rian's still tense, his eyes scanning the room at large, trying to see where the nanobots have been placed.

But my eyes are on the pedestal right in the center of the room.

And the red telephone perched atop it in place of honor.

At the gala on Rigel-Earth, my main goal was acquiring Rian and convincing him that the nanobots had been infected with malware and we needed to do this whole subterfuge.

But I had a personal, secondary goal.

The Museum of Intergalactic History houses a lot of artifacts linked to the development of intergalactic travel. Including, formerly, this red telephone, the same one that was used during the Apollo launches and was once housed at the Mission Control Room in the Houston Space Center way back in the twentieth century. It's an iconic object that was witness to the first steps of humanity in space.

It shouldn't be *here*, in the private collection of the galaxy's richest dumbass, but I suppose that's my fault. I did sort of convince Strom Fetor that he needed the telephone and that it should be right here, and then I maybe manipulated the museum to give it to him after averting a terrorist attack that was actually, for once, not my fault at all. I really didn't get enough credit for that.

Before, I told Rian I don't like strings, but they're not so bad when I'm the one pulling them.

Gotta work quick now.

While Rian's on high alert, looking for the nanobots, my hand snakes out to the telephone on display. I'm a little shocked it's just sitting there. I mean, I did absolutely suggest this very location and rolled the dice that Fetor would obey, but still. If this phone were mine, I'd . . . I don't know, but I wouldn't just put it on a little pedestal in the middle of a room where it's mostly being ignored and not appreciated and where anyone—like me, for example, can pick it up.

"Ada!" Rian hisses when he finally notices what I'm doing. The red receiver is still in my hand. My god, I did *not* expect it to be that easy.

"What?" I ask Rian innocently, tossing the receiver into my other hand, watching the way the coiled cord wiggles.

"Put that back," he says. "We need to find—"

His eyes widen.

I feel the presence of someone behind me.

I set the receiver down slowly, then turn to face Strom Fetor himself.

"Houston," he says, looking down at us, "we have a problem."

# 12

"S trom!" Rian says, attempting to speak with a warm voice that doesn't imply we are absolutely not where we belong.

Fetor only has eyes for me, his face carefully schooled. His gaze slides from me to the red phone and back again.

This is the second time he's caught me touching this phone.

And the second time he's been just a few moments too late to catch what I was *really* doing.

I check my earring, making sure it's secure in my right ear.

*It's fine,* I hum into the subvocal transmitter. I don't look back at Rian as I take a step closer to Fetor, raising both my hands in the air. "Caught me," I say. I let a saucy smile slip over my face, noting the way Fetor's eyes drop to my lips.

Fetor raises an eyebrow. It's a practiced move, I can tell. He thinks he looks intriguing. "Security flagged that you were heading up to your offices, Rian," he says, gaze still pinned on me. "And I when I saw you brought a guest . . ."

"Me." I do a little flair with my hands, framing my face.

"But you're not supposed to be here," he says.

I dare a glance behind the man. There are more people by the door now, wearing dark uniforms. Security goons.

*Ada, we haven't reprogrammed the nanobots!* Rian's panic is evident, even through the computerized voice from the subvocal transmitter. *If you need an hour, we've got to get this started* now, *and we don't even know where the damn things are!*

*It's fine,* I repeat, so low I'm not sure it picks up my words. *Trust me.*

*I* absolutely *do* not *trust you,* Rian shoots back. So, he did hear me.

I take a step forward. Fetor has his hands on his hips, his elbows jutting out, so it's easy for me to slip my fingers through the crook of his arm and steer him around, deeper into the communications building. Out of the corner of my eye, the security guards follow a pace behind. None of the other workers notice us, not really; my plan to just look like I belong would totally have worked if this asshole hadn't interrupted us.

"I know I'm not supposed to be here," I tell Strom. He bends his head toward me, still letting me stroll deeper into the room.

Good. He's amused. Eventually, someone is going to piece together what's happened and tell him, but . . . it's not too late to get out of this whole situation.

"Can you keep a secret?" I ask Fetor.

He pauses. A little smile quirks up one corner of his lips.

"I'm only sleeping with Rian so I can get here," I say in a staged whisper.

Strom snorts, and luckily, the noise cancels out the sputtering sounds Rian makes.

"You didn't seem his type," Fetor says.

What a fucking pretentious jackass.

But I smile sweetly.

"I just have this . . . fascination," I say, gesturing to the room. Everyone here is busy except for us, all the workers bent over consoles or screens or walking with urgency There's a party downstairs, but the people here are too busy ensuring that the entire galaxy's communication network runs smoothly; they don't have time for catered pastries. Unlucky bastards.

"A fascination?" Fetor prompts.

I nod, and while his eyes are glued on me, I notice him wave his hand, letting the security drop back. My heart eases a little, and I funnel that relief into a smile that's actually genuine. "I love the way technology works."

"I guessed. The control room at the museum, the portal ring on display . . ."

"A passion you share with me."

Fetor cocks his head. "I thought you hated me."

I squeeze his elbow. "I *do*," I say. No point lying about

that. "I really despise you. But maybe some of that is jealousy." I force a pout on my lips. *None* of my emotions for Fetor are rooted in envy. "You have all the best stuff. And it's been impossible to see any of it without a little . . ."

"Manipulation?"

I let go of Fetor's arm and snap my fingers as if he said the perfect word. "Exactly!"

Fetor glances at Rian. "Sorry, old boy. I could have told you that you can't trust a girl like her."

"I know," Rian says, glaring.

"Don't be jealous," I say. "We had a good time, didn't we? Consider last week payment for the invite here."

Fetor laughs. He finds this amusing, the idea I'm planting in his head, that I just slept with Rian to get here, next to him.

I am so, so, *so* glad I'm going to fuck him over when he thinks he has a chance to fuck me.

"Anyway," I say, walking deeper into the room, toward an enticingly interesting bank of consoles that all look very important. "I know I shouldn't be here, technically, but—"

"But you're the type of girl who doesn't care about technicalities," Fetor says.

Au contraire, dumbass. But I let him think that.

"Well, you're here now," Fetor says. "This is it—the room where all the magic happens."

By *magic* he means all the communication systems used by the whole galaxy. The nanobots being released today when that fancy holo countdown hits zero outside? They're going to save Earth. But the comm sys? That's . . . everything.

Far, far more valuable.

Far, far more worth stealing.

"Don't run off," Fetor says sharply, turning to Rian, who'd been inching away, trying to break off from us and locate the nanobots. "I can understand wanting to impress your date, but don't think that this isn't still a secure location."

"I expect nothing less," Rian says. Fetor Tech's governmental contracts started here. Probably Fetor was only approved for the climate-cleaner program because he already had the communication-networking contract in place.

Fetor turns his attention back to me. "Well, as you can see, this whole place is quite boring."

I'm not sure if he really means that, but he could not be more wrong. Nothing about any of this is boring. He leads us in an ambling stroll around the entire facility, dismissing the intergalactic receiver hub as "just a booster," and calling the primary communications array a "backup" without seeing the look of shocked displeasure the woman manning that station gives him. He doesn't even know what half the stuff in this room is; he just likes the shiny buttons and pretty blinking lights, and he thinks everyone will be as impressed by it as he is.

For all that Rian says I like to break the law, it should be illegal for any one man to be both this dumb and this rich. It's astounding, really. Any of his employees could run circles around him, but it doesn't take brains to buy stuff. Strom Fetor sees nothing clearly except profit margins.

*The bots aren't here,* Rian tells me subvocally.

*Are you sure?* I ask.

He nods subtly.

Fetor's cuff buzzes, and he pauses, looking at the screen on his wrist. "Time for the real party," he says. "I'll even allow the gate-crasher to come."

As he strides to the door, I meet Rian's panicked eyes. There's no way we can break away from Fetor now.

Even if Rian had been able to locate the nanobots, it's too late.

# 13

Fetor's personal offices overlook Triumph Square. Through the floor-to-ceiling windows we can see the illumination of the countdown displayed for the growing crowd below. The party out there is gearing up to be a rager. We're too far up to hear the thrumming beats of loud music or smell the foods being sold by vendors milling through throngs of people, more's the pity.

"The party's better up here," Fetor tells me. An obvious lie.

But then I spot the chocolate fountain. A glorious display of cascading, creamy chocolate with skewers of fruit and cake just made for dipping. A part of me wants to unhinge my jaw and stand under the direct stream of liquid chocolate, but I don't, because I'm a lady.

Now that we're contained in the office, Fetor moves on to more important guests. A pair of chairs has been set up against the wall, framing the countdown happening outside, and a small woman with braids shepherds him over for an interview as I make a beeline to the food.

This is an even posher spread than the tables the caterers were setting up for the office celebration on floor forty-two. I spot Haoyu Long, and he raises a glass of champagne at me. A server walks by, displaying a bottle with a label from Rian's family's farm. Fetor must have had this shipped in from Rigel-Earth.

Rian sidles up to me. He's a smart man; he knew not to interrupt me until I had dipped into the chocolate fountain.

"We need to get out of here," Rian says in my ear.

He follows my gaze to the door, to the guards in position. If we leave now, it will be noticed.

Rian curses under his breath. "We don't even know where the nanobots were relocated to."

"Mm," I say.

His razor eyes slice right to me. "You're not concerned."

I shrug. "It's too late now. We did our best, but . . ."

A little muscle works in his jaw. "No. That's not it. You should be more concerned."

*He's going to betray you.*

Not if I betray him first.

I can see his mind working. I've turned down food before, when something more important was on the line. His gaze drops from my face to my fingers, where I'm licking off some fruit juice.

Food always gives me away.

"What have you done, Ada?" Rian asks, just loud enough that Haoyu looks up. I smile charmingly at him, and he returns his attention to the chocolate fountain. Smart man.

I spin around to Rian, pulling him into a relatively private corner. The room's not packed, but it's crowded enough that true solitude is impossible. Anyone with a golden ticket to go up the golden elevator cashed it in, and the people allowed guests absolutely brought anyone they could.

But everyone's distracted.

There's a cadre here that truly cares about the program; they're invested in the countdown, eagerly anticipating the launch of the climate cleaners, the salvation of Earth. But they're well outnumbered by the people putting themselves in view of the cam drones or showing off for each other or simply snagging more and more champagne.

The guests here are a mix of the people who care and work, and the people who are on the guest list by nature of being Fetor's friend—and that man only befriends people with high-enough bank accounts.

"Ada," Rian growls, pulling my attention back to him. "I know you would do a lot of things, but giving up isn't one of them."

"Wow, that's kind of eloquent; thank you."

"You know something I don't know," he says.

I smile. "You can't stand it, the not knowing."

"Not when it comes to this," he says, but I replace those words in my head with *Not when it comes to you.*

I glance at the countdown clock. There is less than half an hour left.

Rian grabs my wrist—he doesn't see that I'm trying to look at my cuff, at the totally different countdown timer I started there—and he holds my arms pinned to my sides. It should be uncomfortable, but it's not. He's holding me like I'm the thread leading him out of the labyrinth. Like I'm not just valuable but his whole redemption.

A girl likes to be appreciated.

It's not until I meet his eyes that he speaks. "I can stop it all, right now. I know the optics would be bad. I *will* stop the program before I allow dangerous nanobots to go into Sol-Earth's environment. Ada, tell me what you know. Do I need to kill the countdown?"

I shake back my hair, looking at him a little defiantly. "I know that you shouldn't do that."

"Why." It's more demand than question.

Shit. He's basically cornered me. And while usually that makes me stubborn, right now?

Hot as fuck.

"Okay, so, I told you I needed about an hour or so to reprogram the nanobots, right?" I say. Rian nods. "Well, that's roughly true. But . . ." I get a good look at my cuff's timer. It's hit zero. Rian watches me, focused as I tap the screen and check a little alert that says, *Program Upload Complete.*

"You got to the nanobots?" Rian asks, his voice laced with deadly hope.

I nod. "I *did* need about an hour. But I didn't need to be standing over it the whole time." It's not like I was actively writing the code into the system. Rian knows this. I wrote the whole program already and just needed to install and overwrite the malicious coding Fetor had put into the bots. If he understood the system more, he'd know that all I really needed was to use the fifteen minutes the security system allowed me to do everything I needed to do.

"The nanobots—" Rian starts, but then a little buzzer echoes through the room. All the guests pause, looking around, and Fetor stands up.

He claps once, loud, for attention. "Friends, that sound means that the nanobots have been successfully loaded into the launch site in the communications tower! In moments, it will be time to save Sol-Earth!"

Fucking pretentious asshole—

"Ada," Rian says.

I point to Fetor, and Rian turns, watching as the man moves to a roped-off section in front of the window. A worker wheels out a display stand with a big, shiny red button. Fetor makes a false move, pretending he's going to hit the button early, and people gasp and reporters scramble to get their cam drones positioned for the best shot, but then Fetor laughs mockingly and steps back.

"Soon!" he calls. "For now, drink up!"

Fetor signals for the servers to distribute more bubbly, and he makes a grand show of visiting all his elite guests, a shit-eating grin plastered over his face.

Rian's grip on my arms tightens. "Ada, swear to me that the bots are good now and that the malware is gone."

I look him right in those razored eyes. "I swear to you, your mission was a success."

And so was mine.

"The bots are good?" Urgency threads through every syllable.

I nod and wiggle free from his hold.

"Where do you think you're going?" he asks.

"Chocolate fountain," I say. I mean, obviously. I've showed remarkable restraint so far.

"Saving the world comes first," he growls, pulling me back. I look down at his hand around my elbow, then back up at him, cold as ice. He drops my arm immediately, hands raised in defeat and apology. At least Rian's trainable.

But he doesn't let me leave our little empty spot against the wall. "The nanobots," he says. "Were they—"

"Always in the server room, like you said they would be?" I say. "Yeah, obviously."

Rian's whole hand covers his face as he groans into his

palm, then his fingers glide up his hair, loosening the locks so carefully combed into place.

Oh, I like this. I like to see him unraveling.

I like to be the one doing it.

"You made it sound like they were relocated," he says in a low voice.

I nod. "Yes. Because I lied to you. Honestly, Rian, you should expect that of me by now."

"But then why—"

I'm going to have to spell it out for him. "You wouldn't have snuck me into Fetor's communication tower if you knew I'd already set the program to run. I mean, don't get me wrong, it was a little anxiety-making to do that in fifteen minutes with a computerized voice yelling at me, but in the end, all I had to do was set the program up and walk away. Which I did."

"And then you told me you didn't," Rian said. "Which is a little anxiety-making."

"For you. I knew everything was fine."

"Ada!" My name bursts from him, loud. Several nearby guests turn to look.

Might as well give 'em a show.

I throw my arms around his neck and kiss Rian right on the mouth. He's so surprised that it takes him a moment to register my tongue before his lips part; he deepens the kiss, his arms gripping me around the back, lifting my body and pressing me into the wall. I hear several people nearby chuckle, one woman loudly leading her friend in the opposite direction of us.

Rian's head ducks as his lips trail down my neck, sending a delicious shiver up my spine. "I know you're up to something," he whispers.

I tilt my head back until I hit the wall, exposing more of my neck. Rian's left hand trails from the side of my neck down, fingers pressing into my back, bunching in the fabric as—for a moment—the game turns real, the desire turns liquid. He drags his mouth back up to my ear.

"So, you used me."

I make a noise in the back of my throat—a moan of assent and confirmation. The subvocal transmitter picks it up, and while I don't know what the AI interpreted that sound as, it was enough to make Rian huff in laughter and take a step away.

I grab him by the jacket and pull him back.

Rian cocks an eyebrow at me. His lips are no longer on my skin, but his hands have a mind of their own, trailing up and down my spine, tracing to a low loop before his fingers curl against my hips, needy and desperate.

"I haven't forgotten what you said before," he says. His body may be spiraling into a feral state, but his eyes are clear and sharp.

"Oh?" I say, attempting to be relaxed and failing miserably. "I've forgotten. What did I say?"

He releases my hips, hands going to the wall on either side of my face as he leans over me. "If you wanted to steal something really valuable from a highly secure location, such as, say, the gala at the MIH, you'd just let someone else buy it and steal it from the less-secure location the new owner puts it in."

I can feel the whole length of his body, pinning mine against the wall. This started as a ploy to talk somewhat privately in a room full of guests, but it's rapidly turned into something else. When Rian looks at me now, there is not a single goddamn person in the whole room. It's just him and me and too many clothes between us.

"Did I say that?" My voice is flippant; we both know that's false. "Clever of me."

Rian's eyes narrow, and his lips twitch. "That's you all over, isn't it? Too clever by half."

"I just know how to play the game."

Except do I? Because I'm no longer certain who's the predator and who's the prey.

"This was never a game," Rian says, his voice low, both a threat and a promise.

I open my mouth but he silences me with another kiss, hard and brutal, the kind of kiss that devours, the kind that's not supposed to start in a trumped-up boardroom because it absolutely needs to end somewhere dark and private. This is the kind of kiss that shatters, breaking me up into bite-sized pieces, all the better to eat me.

When Rian rips away from that searing touch, the severing is as violent as the joining. His chest heaves, his lips are bruised and wet, and he is not even a tiny bit satiated.

His forehead bumps into mine, a moment of respite.

"Fuck everything," Rian moans.

"No, just me."

He gives me a little snort of appreciation. "I *know* you're up to something, and I cannot let you get away."

"But you love me."

That earns me a sardonic, deadpan look. "Ada, I know better than to fall for someone like you."

"Someone like me?" I'm all innocence.

"Someone I can never trust. There will always be an angle with you. You will always find a way to use me to your benefit. It would be utterly pointless for me to fall for you."

I swipe a sweaty lock of dark brown hair off the side of his face. "Too late," I whisper. "You already did."

But Rian doesn't rise to the bait. "Ada, I'm serious. You may be doing a bit of a Robin Hood act for me today, stealing from . . ."

He struggles to find the right word. *Rich* isn't strong

enough to describe the type of wealth Strom Fetor wields like an axe.

I offer my own definition. "From an obscenely imbecilic man who crucified his own family to steal a bigger pot of the generational wealth that ensures he never once has to contemplate the deeply corrupt system of oppression that consistently enables him to fail up?"

"Yeah, that works," Rian says. "And I'm with you. Making sure Fetor doesn't win, just this once, when the salvation of all of Earth's citizens is on the lines, that's . . ."

"Noble?" I suggest.

"Close enough to it." He sighs. "But this whole endeavor aside . . . I still believe in the law."

I let my head rest against the cool wall. The more words there are between us, the further we drift from that moment where everything felt like fire in the best possible way. "So, what you're saying is, all I have to do is seduce you with legalese?"

He doesn't even crack a hint of a smile. "I need you to know this: I am going to arrest you."

*You're going to try.*

I can't look him in the eye right now. Instead, my gaze roves over the party, the chocolate fountain, the security, the chocolate fountain.

"You're going to have to face the consequences of your actions," Rian keeps going. "Especially once I . . ."

I feel rather than see Rian's attention drawn to me. Like warm honey down my back, his focus melts into my body.

And I can tell—he's noticed.

Before, my missing earring was on the left side. I left that in the nanobot programming room, stabbing the input receptor with the post and successfully reprogramming the nanobots to protect Earth rather than exploit it.

When I burst out of the server room with the robotic voice telling me that security would be raised in minutes, Rian was too distracted by shutting off the alarms to notice I had no earrings in then.

Which got us to the communications room.

And now I have an earring in the right side.

His eyes shift from my ear to my face. His jaw is tight.

I can see all the pieces falling into place behind his eyes. I can see the accusation just on the tip of his tongue.

And I grin charmingly up at him just as Strom Fetor—and a buzzing cloud of cam drones—walks up to us.

# 14

Except Fetor doesn't stop. A small woman with long twin braids framing her face rushes up, and Fetor leans down to hear something from her. As soon as she's done speaking, he turns on his heel, walking the opposite direction, cam drone floating behind him.

The woman turns to us, braids whipping around. She strides forward with purpose, glaring. At me.

"You have to go," she says.

"Fantastic; I hate it here." I turn to the door, but Rian grabs my wrist. He really is possessive. I'm going to have to do something about that.

"Why?" he asks.

"You can stay, Mr. White," the woman says. I'm assuming from her stance that she's some sort of assistant to Fetor. "But your guest is wearing an article of clothing with flare threads."

My sun shield. It worked to mess with the internal security of the server room, but it's also affecting the cam drones.

Fetor only cares about the nanobot program because he

wants credit. He also wants to be paid in the back end when they fail, but he doesn't know yet that I completely fucked over that agenda. There's a part of me that's pretty thrilled with the idea that I also could mess up the publicity and distract from his little vanity show, but . . .

But I saw the way Rian's spine straightened when the drones were coming. Even now, just being here—there's pride in the way he stands, honor in his pulled-back shoulders.

Mixing a governmental program with private investing rarely works, mostly because of men like Fetor. But doing something this big of scale, something that will truly benefit others . . . that rarely happens. And it's only going to work now because of men like Rian.

And women like me. Funny how there's always someone who does the most but gets no credit, and how that's usually a woman.

"She can take the sun shield off," Rian says.

"That would be fine." The woman nods.

"No, I can just go," I say, mostly to Rian. "I'd rather see the launch from outside. With everyone." Because these are not my people.

"I'll go with you," Rian offers.

"You can stay; it's fine." But I can tell from the way he surveys the room, these are not his people, either.

The woman looks increasingly impatient.

"We'll both go," Rian says, finality ringing in his voice.

"On the one hand, I am going to miss that chocolate fountain," I say. "On the other hand, being in the same room with Strom Fetor is actually putting me off my appetite, so this is for the best."

The woman cracks a smile before she reminds herself to be professional.

"I cannot imagine how you put up with him every day," I tell her.

"He does pay well," she allows.

"Come *on*," Rian says.

He escorts me past security—always easier to get out than in—and to the golden elevators. We drop rapidly and without interruption; this lift doesn't deign to stop on other floors just because some common person pushed a call button.

"So," I say, watching the numbers flick by on the screen as we descend.

"So."

I glance at Rian. He looks almost as nervous now as he did before I stepped into the server room.

"What's next?" I ask. Quiet.

He doesn't meet my eyes.

I know an arrest wasn't likely to happen in Strom Fetor's party office with dozens of live feeds being recorded. It wasn't just the publicity of the event; Rian wouldn't want to taint his triumph with . . . well, with me.

The golden doors slide open, depositing us in the lobby.

We have to scan through again, our ident sequences registering our departure.

We step out into the bright, sunny day and are immediately assaulted by noises and smells and *vibrancy*. Fetor Tech was remarkably soundproofed, and the tinted glass dulled the reality outside. Chocolate fountains are great, sure, but steps away I can see fresh fruit being hawked, hover cars full of frozen concoctions, a fry station that's doing something decadent with peppers, and people walking around with sticks holding wrapped treats, sweet and savory—slices of halva, skewers of meat dumplings, bags of spiced nuts. A myriad of voices wrap around everything—not everyone speaking in Standard, but real languages, the stuff people use at home, the words steeped in culture and experience. There's laughter and music and life.

And thousands—millions—of eyes all point up at the countdown holo projected in front of the skyscraper.

I whirl around to Rian.

He looks . . . sad.

I grab his hands. "Right, okay, you're going to make an attempt to arrest me," I say.

"I'm going to—"

"You're going to try," I give him that much. "Meanwhile, there's less than fifteen minutes left before the nanobots are released. There's a whole party down here. And we've both of us worked too hard not to take advantage of it."

He hesitates.

I press my luck. "So—just for the next fifteen minutes—can we pretend this is all normal? That we did a good thing and we can both celebrate?"

I think he can tell what I'm really asking for: *Can we pretend that the countdown won't end with the end of us?*

He stares into my eyes and finally, finally nods.

"Excellent!" I clap and dive into the fray. "Let's also pretend this is a date."

"Better than our first date," Rian says. He has to shout to be heard over the crowd, so some of the impact is lost.

"I still maintain that kidnapping is memorable!" I call back cheerily. "Also, if this is a date, that means you're paying." I wave over a person selling blocks of imqaret and force Rian to scan his cuff for a pair.

Rian reaches for the second imqaret, but I bat his hand away. "Get your own," I tell him, but the person who was selling them has already drifted into the crowd, disappearing. I see Rian connect that to me—how easy it would be for me to fade into this chaotic crowd. He takes two big steps closer, ignoring me when I reluctantly offer him a bite of the date-filled pastry.

He's not going to let me out of his sight.

There are uniformed officers sprinkled throughout the crowd—quite a few, actually, more than normal. I wonder if Rian enlisted them or if they're just here because a crowd is here, and crowds on festa days aren't always peaceful.

When I try to push deeper into the throng of people, Rian stays right beside me. I swing into a chaotic dance with strangers, and he stubbornly refuses to move from his position right in the way.

It's not just him.

I thought I was merrily skittering through the crowd, but it takes me only a few minutes to realize I'm seeing the same faces. The woman with bushy, curly red hair. The tall person in the navy-blue tunic. The man with painted designs on his bald head, a swirl of rainbow colors.

Every time I turn, I see them. Their faces are tilted to me like sunflowers soaking up the sun.

Watching.

Waiting.

These are Rian's people.

And all around me I can see the net closing, tighter and tighter.

In a crowd this large, I shouldn't recognize anyone, but— the middle-aged woman wearing holo glasses, the couple by the view ring, and even Phoebe, whose hat doesn't block her identity.

I whirl around, spotting more faces. And when I turn again, Rian fills my vision.

The crowd is so loud, I can barely hear him, but I see him pointing up at the holo countdown.

All around, the people start chanting, caught up in the moment.

*Ten! Nine!*

I take in a breath.

*Eight! Seven!*

Let it out.

*Six! Five!*

I pull Rian's face to mine. This kiss isn't hungry or needy.

*Four! Three!*

It's a goodbye.

# 15

*Two!*

I open my eyes just in time.

*One!*

Holo-casts shoot up, glittering in a dazzling display of light visible even under the shining Mediterranean sun, swirling in patterns—waves, I think, artistically rendered in a rainbow of colors.

The actual launch of the nanobots is almost anticlimactic. A poof of a cloud, a wisp of barely visible smoke from a short pipe extending from the communication tower atop Fetor's skyscraper. The white puff evaporates in seconds, although the sparkling holo-casts burst out even brighter.

"Ada," Rian says. His hand is around my wrist. I quickly scan the crowd—the net is tightening. I thought I was moving randomly throughout the square, but I'm actually off to the side, close to the Central Gardens gate.

"Look!" someone nearby shouts.

And everyone does. That's what happens when people in a crowd start pointing to the sky and shouting *Look!*

People look.

Even Rian.

A flock of messenger birds swoops over Triumph Square.

The exact same gray as the feather that came with the box I got this morning.

"Thanks, Mom," I mutter as I raise my sun shield's hood over my face.

And, all around me, hundreds—thousands—of people do the same.

Rian may have peppered his people throughout the crowd, and they may have been circling around us like vultures, waiting for the right time to claim me.

But he's not the only one to spike the crowd with allies.

Mom's pigeons are not just pets. They're messengers. And they've just told every single person sympathetic to Earth's salvation to help me disappear.

This isn't official business. Mom is like me—she keeps her circle tight. But just like Bruna's cousin gave Rian and me a ride to the city this morning, it's not hard to whisper from friend to friend to wear sun shields with flare threads and raise them when the birds fly. I bet ninety percent of the people here consider this little more than a flash-mob stunt, but they're willing to participate for their impassioned cousin, their idealistic best friend, the sheer chaos of it all.

Still, this many people? All coming to help me? This is the legacy my mother has given this planet. That when push comes to shove, when she lets it be known in secret codes and silent whispers that she needs help—the people rise to help. Every single person on this island—with the obvious exception of Strom Fucking Fetor—knows that the work my mother does helps others, even if they don't know Mom personally.

Emotion clogs my throat. This? This is more powerful than the secrets I have in my earring.

Not more easily sold on the black market, though, and that's the difference between my mother and me.

I've got my sun shield over my head, but Rian's not yet let go of my wrist. He turns from the soaring birds to my face, immediately clocking the way I've pulled the hood up, how I'm reaching into my pocket for eye protectors.

"Now!" Rian shouts, his hand crushing my wrist in a vise-like grip. He doesn't know what's coming, but he can read the signs; he can tell I'm doing something. *"NOW!"*

His net tightens. His people push through the crowd, ignoring the angry shouts of others.

Above, the messenger birds swirl in front of the crowd.

And then they explode.

I mean, not really. Mom would never let her precious pigeons just blow up. But they must have had a flash bomb attached to their legs or something, released remotely, I don't know. That was Mom's job. And it worked. Because as soon as I have the dark lenses over my eyes, the flash bomb goes off, a flare of brilliant, pure-white light.

It's the middle of the day, so its effects are pretty limited, but if, say, you happened to be looking right at someone wearing a sun shield laced with flare threads, then yeah, you're going to get blinded.

By instinct, Rian drops my wrist to cover his eyes.

At least half the crowd mimics the way he tosses an arm over his face. Because when the pigeons flew overhead, that was the first sign. All the people seeded into the crowd on my side—Mom's side—raised their hoods and covered their faces, and anyone who happened to be looking at them got a blindingly bright flash straight into their retinas.

The result is chaos.

Exactly as planned.

Thousands of people are all dressed exactly like me—in clothing so bright, no one can look at us. And there's no better time to disappear when the one you're running from can't even look at you.

I spin on my heel and push through the crowd. Rian immediately shouts my name, but I don't pause. I spare him only one look back. He gropes blindly, blinking rapidly, trying to clear his vision.

"Move out!" Rian shouts, and the people in the crowd who work for him attempt to recover and chase me. But between the spots that no doubt still block their vision and the fact that huge swaths of the crowd are wearing the exact same sun shield as me, I'm able to slip through. I spot people being grabbed, hoods ripped off, but the disguise is enough for me to make it through the crowds.

I charge under a view ring. Before, the floating screens showed various different areas of Earth or cities from other planets. Now more than half of them display white—not because the screens were hacked, but because the people on the other side of the portal are holding white shirts, blank images, or empty pieces of paper up to the lenses. Mom must have been able to reach agents throughout the galactic system to come out and further add to the chaos. Sure enough, just when the woman with bushy red hair locks eyes with me, I dodge in front of a view-ring screen, and the white glow is enough to make her wince in pain and look away as the light catches the flare threads of my sun shield.

If I think too much about how Mom's network has reached throughout the galaxy, how one person's altruistic goal to just *help* others inspired people from multiple planets to show up and help, I'll collapse under the weight of it all.

Instead, I focus on running. This disguise won't work forever—I have only chaos and confusion on my side right now.

"That way!" a man with dark skin, his sun-shield hood raised, points for me, gesturing for me to skirt the edge of Central Gardens as I leave Triumph Square. His friends have cheap flashlights, and they shine them at each other, brilliant flashes of light from their reflective clothing enough to distract my pursuers from the way I race around the corner.

My feet thunder over the moving walkway. There are fewer people here, but most of them are moving in the opposite direction, toward the square.

I risk a glance behind me.

As soon as I cut through the foot traffic, the people fill in the holes I made. Sun shield hoods are raised again. More flashlights.

My heart makes a funny thump as I leap off the walkway and veer to the right, to the edge of the city. A high wall keeps people from leaping off the side of the bridge New Venice is built upon, but a bank of lifts and an emergency stairwell go back down to the water. If I can just get there—

A person in a sun shield motions me to go to the elevator door on the corner; they're holding it for me. I throw myself inside, lungs gasping for air from my frantic race through the crowd.

Moments before the doors slide shut, I see Rian and a group of his agents pushing through the crowd, knocking people off the moving walkway. His razor-sharp eyes pause, taking it all in: all the people wearing sun shields, all the bodies conveniently clustering around him, slowing him down, the flashlights that flare brightly and blind him and his team.

It's as if all the world were here today not to watch the release of the nanobots but to help me escape.

# 16

Bruna meets me on the platform. "Did they see you?" she asks, already leading me around to the back, away from the public, tourist-facing area to where the workers gather.

"I don't think so," I gasp.

Above us, all the lift lights illuminate. Whether Rian saw me get in the elevator or not, he sent people down here.

"Quick." Bruna shoves a helmet at me. The front is clear, and it seals around my face. The back is a breather unit. As soon as I've got the helmet on, a digital display in the top of my vision informs me that I have an hour of oxygen.

"And this," Bruna adds.

"How did you get my jetpack?" Because this is *my* jetpack—the jaxon jet that burns cold and never fails me, except when I design it to fail.

Bruna gives me a look I recognize from our college days, a look that tells me to shut the fuck up and just accept the help I'm given. She's the port boss, and she got me the jets. "Thanks," I tell her, and she grunts in a way I know means, *You're welcome but also hurry the fuck up.*

I shrug my jetpack onto my shoulders and strap the stabilizer around my waist. The unit is designed to work with my LifePack; it's designed to work in space. But as soon as I secure the gear, Bruna shoves me into the Mediterranean Sea.

Blue darkness washes over me as my body sinks underwater. Panic sweeps into my lungs, but the helmet Bruna gave me keeps placidly pumping air. I gulp at it, my heart hammering, and I am able to refocus enough to kick down, not up. Down and out. Away from the boats and the platforms under the city.

Away from Rian.

"Ada?" a voice says in my helmet.

"Mom?"

"Hey, honey." Relief threads through my mother's voice. "You have the coordinates?"

Even before she has the sentence out, I notice a dial at the top of the helmet's screen, a little radial that blinks when I veer too far off course.

"It'll take you to the landing strip, but try not to surface before then," Mom says. "And don't use the jets until you're at least half a kilometer from the island."

If I surface now, there's a chance Rian will have scouters watching the water. I'll be caught. Using my jetpack to propel through the ocean might also be spotted; I'm not *that* deep underwater, and Rian isn't going to exactly give up easily.

That thought—of him scanning the waves, of him searching for me—shouldn't excite me quite the way it does.

I focus on swimming, avoiding the bits of trash and trying not to think about how gross the water is. Even now, some of the nanobots have to be here, replicating themselves, isolating the pollutants to form globules that can easily be removed and recycled into cleaner components.

"Hey, Mom," I say. "Thanks."

"Always," Her word is a whisper, and I can barely hear it as I continue swimming, my breath increasingly ragged from effort. But it still fills me with warmth. Maybe the only reason I am willing to take the risks I do is because Mom's always been there to catch me when I fall. It's easier to walk a tightrope when you know there's a safety net beneath your wobbly feet.

Her love gives me courage. It always does, even when I know she's lightyears away. And maybe if I wasn't hauling ass through the sea, I'd find the words to tell her that. I hope she knows anyway. I suspect she does.

She always knows more than I give her credit for. Like how she knew not to rely on regular communication systems for this. Rian *had* to have had people monitoring all the networks.

Can't monitor birds and whispers, though.

I wait until my helmet flashes green to use the jetpack. The swim goes much quicker with that little aid.

"I'm almost there," I tell Mom as I approach the dock. "Where are you?"

"Safe." That's the only answer I'm going to get from her. She and I have both learned to never really trust any comm sys.

We'll find each other again. We always do.

I breach the surface of the water and spot the ladder going up to the platform. My skin stinks with the sticky-salty water that comes off me in sheets as I lug my body, weighed down with the jetpack, up onto the station platform.

There's no one here to help me, but that's fine. Bruna's the port boss, and while she set me up with my escape route, either she's told the other workers on the dock to ignore me or they're sympathetic enough to turn a blind eye as I trudge over to *Glory*.

I don't risk anything—I get into my pilot seat still dripping wet, not bothering to take the time to change clothes. I swipe my damp hair out of my face and drop the breathing helmet in the seat Rian occupied when we came to Earth.

In minutes, I'm in the air, soaring north to avoid the lingering holo-casts that paint the sky with colorful light.

Ships are supposed to be grounded now. If Rian is looking in my direction, he'll know that the streak of light escaping Earth's gravity is me.

He'll know I got away.

Not because I'm clever—at least not this time.

But because the people of Earth are tired—have been tired, for generations—of being trod upon, ignored, and used. Because when there was a chance to exact some level of justice, all they needed was a sign to rise up.

# 17

don't stop until Mars.

I take the short portal across the solar system, using the codes my mother helped me acquire. I get far enough away, in other words, that I could tell Rian my exact location and he wouldn't be able to get to me in at least a week, and then only if he were lucky.

I didn't just sit there while in the portal. Of course. I had work to do.

First thing first: Extract all the data from my earring.

I spent a shit ton of cash on these suckers, and I had to leave one behind in Fetor's server room. Worth it, I suppose, since jamming the post into the nanobot programmer enabled my code to overwrite his. Eventually, maybe, someone will notice a random stray earring. But I'm already half a solar system away.

The other earring?

Far more valuable.

*This* was the thing I got out of the red telephone, after hiding it there at the gala. Rian had the right idea but the wrong execution. He thought that I was going to steal the red phone, and that I needed Fetor to move it to a less-secure location for me to do that.

That was never the plan.

The plan was to hide this earring in the phone, something that took me only seconds, thanks to its narrow design. I planted it while still at the gala at the Museum of Intergalactic History.

Its tiny size was why the earring was so expensive in the first place. It's a wireless scanner and recorder. And before I put it in the red telephone from NASA, I had it programmed to scan for a specific code.

This is where the plan fell to luck and timing, but for once, I actually did get lucky here. I got the phone to Fetor, who took my suggestion to put it in the communication room. And with the scanner in the room, it had time to infiltrate the system and copy every line of code I would need to break in to the entire communications network.

It took me the entire journey from Earth to Mars to parse it out, and there are bits that I'm still not sure about. I'd already written several programs to help extract the data I needed, though, and that helped speed the process along.

When I reach Mars, the first thing I do is line up a portal code. Just in case Rian has people out here, in this remote corner of the system. It's unlikely, but . . .

The next thing I do is hack in to security feeds.

See, people don't realize how much of a role communication networks play. All the cam drones? They don't *store* the data they record. It travels via communication networks into a server that's backed up remotely to other servers.

The communication network is a road that will take me through any locked door.

Top of the list: Strom Fetor's security-access feeds. Once I get into the comm sys, it's surprisingly easy to bring up all the footage.

Rian and I were spotted in the communication room, but Fetor didn't know we'd made a stop in the server room. And now he never will. I scrub all the records of Rian accessing the room and delete the video feeds of me—in my blinding-white flare threads—inside it. I also track down the footage from the stairwell and slice that out, too. By the time I'm done, I have laid the digital groundwork for a perfectly normal visit to the towers. And, more important, all the plausible deniability Rian will need when Fetor inevitably figures out that someone has reprogrammed the bots he intended to be a cash cow for the rest of Earth's history.

I am absolutely certain that Fetor's simply not intelligent enough to link me to any of this, especially if I clear Rian. The man has many enemies, corporate and personal. But he does hire smart people, and so I have little doubt that eventually, my name will be one of the few remaining on his list of suspects. Maybe then he'll finally believe I actually really hate him.

I don't delete the footage of me in the communication room.

Maybe I should. Pride before a fall and all that.

But I like the idea of him searching and searching, not knowing who reprogrammed the bots, until some overworked and underpaid person presents him with a shot of me extracting the earring from the red telephone he so graciously put on a pedestal right in front of me.

He'll never make this public. He'll never admit to the galaxy how easy it was for me to strip him of the very data that turned him from a billionaire to a trillionaire.

And by the time he realizes it was me, I'll be a ghost.

Untraceable.

If Fetor was a more intelligent man, he'd look into using messenger pigeons in the future.

Once I ensure Fetor Tech has no damning evidence of what we did, I go into the government records. It takes longer to break into them, but they have the same flaw. Everything goes through the comm network.

I meticulously root out every iteration of me and my mother and delete it. Then I go into all the records of Green Rogue—what a ridiculous code name for the movement—

and seed in plenty of lies, misinformation, and false leads to give everyone a bit of cover for the next few years.

My mother didn't approve of the risk I was taking to get access to the communications system. But she extricated me anyway, blowing her cover and cashing in all the goodwill she's built for decades to aid me.

Least I can do in return. Besides, next time, I can charge her more. Maybe I'll even toss a little spy bot to her underground network on the house. I'm feeling generous these days.

I crack my knuckles as I lean back in my chair. Through the carbonglass window, I can see the round, red curvature of Mars. Closer to me is the portal.

It's time to disappear forever.

# UNITED GALACTIC SYSTEM

## MEMO

From: Rian C. White, DoIBiTe
To: All Personnel, All Departments
Subject: Climate-Cleaner Launch
*Attachments:* Report CJB3

It is with tremendous pride to my whole team that I can announce that the Climate-Cleaner Project launched successfully! Early reports indicate that the nanobots are efficiently operating at prime levels, and there is already evidence on a microscopic level tracking positively. Please see attached our hopeful projection of Sol-Earth ecological recovery.

Of course, we all know that cleaning up Sol-Earth's water cycle will take years, even with these effective measures, but we expect to see visible changes within the next twelve to twenty-four months.

This was truly a team effort, and no one person[1] can be credited with the successful launch. Together, we are saving Sol-Earth, one water molecule at a time!

---

1   A lie. This would not have succeeded without Ada Lamarr.

---

## SUBJECT: XLENDI TOWER

From: Phoebe Brücke, Doll
To: Rian C. White, DolBiTe

Rian,

My team and I went to the location you gave us. Xlendi Tower showed no sign of occupation. While the main floor still held historical artifacts and tourism displays, the bottom floor, which you indicated was living quarters, was completely devoid of any personal belongings or signs of life.[1] There was not even food in the cabinets. The roof of the tower had solar panels and an empty wooden structure that seems to have housed birds.[2] [3]

---

1   How did Ada get the tower empty so fast? She couldn't have. This must be Jane evacuating while Ada and I were at Fetor Tech. Which means . . . Jane knew Ada would be doing something nefarious.

2   She even took the damn birds?

3   But why did *Jane* run? Even if Ada warned her, *Jane* had no reason to flee. At best, we would have questioned her, but Ada knows I wouldn't arrest her mother for something she did. Unless . . . No. *Fuck.* Impossible. But . . . Ada was so quick to make me think "Jane" was a family name, not a link to . . .

# UNITED GALACTIC SYSTEM

**SUBJECT: GREEN ROGUE / JANE IRWIN**
**MARKED: TOP SECRET**
*Highest level of encryption*

From: Rian C. White, DoIBiTe
To: Jamie Nix, DoII

Jamie,

In regards to the suspect we spoke of earlier, I'm having trouble finding some records that I wanted to follow up on. You know I've been trying to locate information on Ada Lamarr, and the records have clearly been tampered with.

Separately, I'm trying to find more information on her mother.

First name: Jane.

Last name: presumed to be Lamarr.[1]

Last known whereabouts: Xlendi Tower, Malta (Gozo)

Prior known locations: Yellowstone Park, United States of America (before volcano; worked as a ranger through the private tourism board.)

---

1  Why didn't I confirm this sooner? I got distracted. Like Ada wanted me to be.

I have a lead that indicates Jane worked within the government, and have since been trying to locate definitive information on her but am having trouble. I figured this was more in your department. Let me know if you'd like me to file a formal request for information, but time is short on this.

# UNITED GALACTIC SYSTEM

## SUBJECT: RE: GREEN ROGUE / JANE IRWIN
## MARKED: TOP SECRET
### *Highest level of encryption*

From: Jamie Nix, Doll
To: Rian C. White, DolBiTe

Rian,

Well, Jane Lamarr is certainly a ghost. You know more than I do. I went into Yellowstone records and couldn't even find her there. Following up on Ada Lamarr's ident sequence and birth records, no mother is listed.[1] There's not even a hospital record of anyone being in the room when Ada was born. Whoever scrubbed Jane Lamarr from the records was *thorough.*[2]

---

1 What the fuck? I looked up those records when I was screening Ada for security at the gala. I *know* I saw both her parents' names listed on the birth records.

2 Fuckfuckfuckfuck, I'm pretty sure I know who did *that.*

# UNITED GALACTIC SYSTEM

**SUBJECT: RE: RE: GREEN ROGUE / JANE IRWIN**
**MARKED: TOP SECRET**
*Highest level of encryption*

From: Rian C. White, DolBiTe
To: Jamie Nix, Doll

Jamie,

It seems likely that Ada Lamarr scrubbed her mother's records in the time between the gala, when I last accessed them, and now. It is unfortunate that I did not keep offline records of what I read, but I do recall there being more, which means that our files have been tampered with. Please advise in regards to securing the records from being further tampered with through hacking.

# UNITED GALACTIC SYSTEM

## MEMO

From: Jamie Nix, Doll
To: All Personnel, All Departments
Subject: WARNING: HACKED SYSTEMS

Be advised:

It has come to our attention that various records within the system have been tampered with. There has been a breach of security that we are actively working to fix.[1]

---

1 If we only knew *how* the security was broken. What the hell did Ada do?!

# UNITED GALACTIC SYSTEM

**MARKED: TOP SECRET**
**ENCRYPTED CHAT LOG: CONFIRMED SECURE**

**RIAN WHITE**: Phoebe, any additional data on Xlendi Tower?

**PHOEBE BRÜCKE**: There's a record of someone working there for the tourism department, but not Jane Lamarr or Jane anything.

**RW**: I assumed as much.

**PB**: It may be obvious, but . . . Jane Lamarr . . . Jane Irwin . . .

**RW**: Are you thinking they may be the same person?[1]

**PB**: It's possible, right? We don't know who leads the Green Rogue organization. It *could* be Ada's mother.

**RW**: Considering Jane disappeared from Xlendi Tower so quickly, and the fact that all information has been scrubbed

---

1  Because it seems obvious *now*.

from records that are *highly* classified and supposed to be secure . . .[2]

**RW:** Yeah, the thought has crossed my mind as well.

**PB:** We all thought Ada was personally invested in saving Earth because of her father's death.[3]

**RW:** But she'd be personally invested if her mother was leading the top-secret organization "protecting" Sol-Earth, too.

**PB:** Yeah.

<<Networking Connection Error>>

<<User *Phoebe Brücke* has been removed from secure chat.>>

**UNKNOWN:** Hi, Rian.

**RW:** Who is this?

**UNKNOWN:** Do I need to spell it out for you?

**RW:** Ada.

**UNKNOWN:** :)

---

2  Plus the birds that were used as a distraction . . .

3  Climate sickness. Another reason for her to hate Fetor, too, because he sat on the vaccine so long, her father was never able to get treatment.

**RW:** WHAT THE ACTUAL FUCK, ADA?!

**UNKNOWN:** Okay, you're mad.

**RW:** WHAT HAVE YOU DONE???

**UNKNOWN:** You're so dramatic.

**UNKNOWN:** But also, need I point out that I don't have any information that the government hasn't already granted Strom Fetor?[4]

**UNKNOWN:** I'm just smart enough to use it.

**RW;** WHERE ARE YOU?

**UNKNOWN:** Just outside a portal.

**RW:** Which one?

**UNKNOWN:** I'm *not* going to tell you which portal, silly. Just know I'm going to skip around the whole galaxy for a bit. Got some exploring to do.

**RW:** So . . . what? You used me to get into the communications network? That about it?

**UNKNOWN:** . . .

**RW:** You can't get away with this, Ada. You're playing with the *government* now.

**UNKNOWN:** Oooo, scary.

---

4  That's another security hole I'm going to have to flag Jamie with.

**RW:** ADA.

**UNKNOWN:** RIAN.

**RW:** You know I can't just let this slide.

**RW:** You know I'm going to have to arrest you. For real. It won't be trumped-up kidnapping charges.

**RW:** These are serious crimes, Ada.

**UNKNOWN:** Oh, I know.

**UNKNOWN:** But you know what else I know?

**RW:** What?

**UNKNOWN:** I know you love the chase.[5]

**UNKNOWN:** Almost as much as you love me.[6]

**UNKNOWN:** And if you want me, you're going to have to come and get me.[7]

---

5  Fuck, I do.

6  *Fuck*, I do.

7  Oh, I will.

## ACKNOWLEDGMENTS

Once, when I was far younger and far, far more naïve, I went abroad with my mother. During that time, we went walking together through the streets of Venice, notorious for the number of pigeons littering the historical square. The birds were accustomed to treating tourists like me with an eye of caution, but through a series of mishaps, I happened to startle one at the best/worst time possible, and a pigeon flew up the skirt of a stranger walking in front of us. The poor woman screamed—having a bird fly frantically toward your nether regions isn't exactly comforting—and my mother and I broke down in such maniacal laughter that we fell over on a nearby stoop, absolutely howling. To this day, all I have to do to make my mother laugh until she cries is bring up that bird.

I used to think that the pigeon was nothing more than a senseless tool in the comedic relief of a family legend, but as I grew older, I learned the role humans played in the domestication and then abandonment of pigeons. As I worked on

Ada's master plan to hack into the communication network of the galaxy, I started thinking about how communication has changed over the years. And Jane Lamarr and her messenger pigeons wormed their way into the story.

So, thank you, random pigeon, for creating an indelible memory. And sorry, random woman who I inadvertently probably gave a bird phobia to. This book would not exist the way it is without the chance encounter of that bird under that skirt with me as witness (and instigator, let's be real) to the event.

From turning that seed of a decades-old memory into a novel with heists and twists, I also have to thank my agent, Merrilee Heifetz, and her assistant, Rebecca Eskildsen, for their constant support and belief in Ada.

Of course, I could also not do any of this without the brilliant aid of the entire DAW team. Navah Wolfe has kept all the chaotic threads of Ada's story in line, and her loving notes to make the story better or to comment on how hot Rian's romance with Ada is filled me with joy. Ada Lamarr is a fictional character smarter than her author, and Navah's guidance in helping me pick apart the strands of her secrets is invaluable. Madeline Goldberg keeps both of us organized, Elizabeth Koehler has managed the production of the book, and Joshua Starr has helped make the messy footnotes and weird formatting I thrust upon this story actually make sense and look good for you, the reader. Laura Fitzgerald,

Elena Stokes, and Briana Robinson have gone above and beyond to help ensure this book gets into your hands. As always, thanks also to Betsy Wollheim, who has made DAW books into a home for both writers and readers.

I also want to say a beloved thanks to Wordsmith Workshops, who ~~cyberbullied me~~ cheered me on to finish writing this manuscript in time. Special shout-out to author Scott Tracey, who helped me come up with the name Strom Fetor.

My heart to my family: my son, who told me I was only allowed to write during his sport practices if I promised to take him to Disney World, and my husband, who tried to contain the tiny gremlin from crawling all over me while I pounded away at the keyboard. We should probably go to Disney World now.

Love to my mother: you've been fucking brilliant while I fucking cussed a lot, which I know you fucking hate, but I fucking love you anyway. And just because she told me I should have censored my language, I will leave you, Mom, with the last word:

F.